BOOK FOUR

jessica's wish

Cover design by Okay Creations
Book layout by Lori Colbeck

ISBN-13: 978-1-950348-09-1

STONEHILL
BOOK FOUR

jessica's wish

MARCI
BOLDEN

PINK SAND
PRESS

PROLOGUE

*a*s the candles on her birthday cake flickered, Jessica Martinson-Canton closed her eyes. Eleven. Eleven candles meant this wish would be even stronger than all the others. She took a breath and asked for the same thing she'd wanted for as long as she could remember—*I wish I had a mom*.

She opened her eyes and blew out the candles with one big breath.

Everyone cheered as if she'd done something great. She wasn't sure if that was because she was the only kid in the family —the only *biological* kid anyway; there were plenty of what her dad called "Grandma's strays"—or if they were overreacting because she had Down syndrome. Blowing out birthday candles didn't really call for applause, but they were as excited now as they had been when she'd performed in the school play. She'd been a tree, just like Jasper Townsend—the girl who moved to

Stonehill from someplace far away and couldn't speak English very well yet.

Since they were trees, neither of them said any lines, but they did get to change costumes because each act was a new season. That was fun. Even though they didn't really understand each other, they had giggled at how they had to hurry up and take off one tree and put on another.

Her grandpa had said Jessica was a natural actress. Jessica thought he was doing what her dad called blowing smoke, which she'd figured out meant someone was lying just to be nice. Her grandma did that a lot, too, but Jessica didn't mind because when her grandparents said nice things, they made her heart feel good.

Her mom had left when Jessica was a baby. Her dad always tried to make up excuses why, but Jessica was smart enough to know the truth. Her mom didn't want a baby with Down syndrome. If Jessica thought about that too much, she'd feel so sad she'd cry, so she tried to always focus on the good things.

Besides, after her mom left, Grandma took care of Jessica while her dad finished school and got a job. Grandma was the greatest artist Jessica had ever seen and was able to stay home and make sure Jess never fell too far behind the other kids.

Her dad thought Grandma was irresponsible, but Jessica didn't think so. Grandma was just free-spirited. Jessica thought that made her fun.

As the clapping continued, Jessica rolled her eyes but couldn't help the grin that spread across her face. Even if she had just blown out a few candles, hearing everyone so happy for her made her feel happy, just like when Grandpa blew smoke.

Her grandma rocked another one of those babies who wasn't related to them against her chest in a long pink elephant-covered papoose so the baby didn't fuss. Then her grandpa scooped homemade ice cream while her dad cut the cake.

Jessica had wanted a cake with her favorite singer on it, but Grandma didn't like processed sugars and chemicals. Grandma made the cake herself and covered it with purple icing and pretty pink writing, which Jessica figured were all-natural. Her dad pulled out the slice he cut for her, and all of a sudden the boring old cake turned into something magical.

Jessica gasped. Her grandma was watching her reaction like she always did. Sometimes Jessica exaggerated her excitement because she knew that made her grandma happy, but this time, she didn't have to act. She really was surprised and *so* happy.

"Wow," she whispered as multi-colored candies fell like confetti from the cake. They weren't the grocery store kind of candies—those would never pass Grandma's inspection—but they were still candies. Jessica popped a pink one into her mouth and smiled when chocolate melted on her tongue.

This was the best cake *ever*. She knew then that it was a sign. This was the year...the year her wish would finally come true.

CHAPTER ONE

*P*hil Martinson-Canton eased onto the plush sofa in his parents' living room while his mother perched on a wooden rocking chair and cooed to the whining baby. Kara had raised Phil on her own—his father hadn't come into the picture until Phil was an adult. Instead of having a "normal" life, Kara and Phil had spent the better part of his youth in communes for single mothers. She now felt it was her duty to support every broken family she stumbled upon—including taking in babies like Mira when the need arose. Kara had always been a baby whisperer, but this particular infant seemed resistant to her maternal nature.

Though Phil had stopped to visit under the pretense of inviting his parents to lunch, he'd sent his daughter to help her grandpa heat up a bottle so he could talk privately with his mother. He hated confronting Kara when she looked so exhausted, but she had a way of worming her way into areas of his life where she had no business being. Her meddling had always been tiresome, but now he was a grown man with a child of his own. He found it intolerable, and he needed to put a stop to it.

"Jessica is at it again," he said.

Kara creased her brow at him. "At what?"

"She's been talking about me dating her teacher, Mom. As though it's going to happen."

"Why are you looking at me like that's my fault?"

Phil frowned at her. She knew *exactly* why that was her fault. "You've been giving me a really hard time about being single."

She had the gall to look offended. "I have not."

"Yes, you have."

"Your mom is just worried about you." Harry walked into the living room shaking a baby bottle. Phil's dad always made excuses for Kara. She hated seeing Phil lonely. She wanted Jessica to have a mother figure in her life. As far as Phil was concerned, neither of those excuses justified planting the seed in Jessica's head that her dad needed a girlfriend...especially if Kara had implied that Jessica's teacher should be that girlfriend.

"Where's Jess?" Phil asked, not wanting to hash this out in front of her.

"She said she wanted a glass of water, but your mom made cookies this morning. I'm sure we're going to be missing a few when you leave."

Phil opened his mouth to protest—they were headed to the

café for lunch—but if Jess was sneaking snacks, at least she'd be occupied. Returning his attention to his mother, he got the conversation back on track. "Jess thinks I was *flirting* with her teacher."

"Were you?" Harry handed Kara the warm bottle of formula.

"*No.*"

Harry grinned, mischief sparkling in his eyes. "I wouldn't blame you. That is one good-looking elementary school teacher."

Phil gawked at his mother as she situated Mira in the crook of her arm. "Did you hear that?"

Kara casually shrugged. "Well, she is good-looking. If I were younger and single—"

"Oh my God, Mother." Phil closed his eyes while his parents laughed. Blowing out some of his frustration between his lips, he pressed his palms together and tightly entwined his fingers, willing himself to remain calm. "Look, the last thing I need is my daughter telling people I flirt with her teacher. Good grief, what if she told her classmates that? Eleven-year-old girls aren't exactly known for keeping secrets. Shit," he said thoughtfully. "Maybe that's why Ms. Jackson acted so nervous at our last conference."

His parents laughed again, and he glared at them.

Kara had long ago embraced a bohemian style. She never seemed overly concerned with styling her long strawberry-blond hair, but as she rolled her head back, he noted how the messy bun on top of her head had become just as much a part of her style as brightly colored long skirts and fitted T-shirts. The exhaustion no longer showed only in dark bags under her eyes. His father's dark hair seemed grayer by the day and the lines around his mouth somehow deeper.

Caring for this baby was starting to impact his parents on a level he'd never seen before. His concern for their wellbeing would wait for another day, however. Right now, he just needed his mother to stop interfering in his personal life.

"Mom. I'll date when I'm ready. Please, no more."

"No more what?" Kara asked. "What exactly do you think I've been doing, Phil?"

"You tried to set me up on no fewer than three dates last month. And in front of Jess."

"All I asked was if you were interested in going out with my friend's daughter."

"Three times. In front of Jessica."

Kara frowned in that way she always did when he confronted her about her behavior. They'd butted heads from the time Phil could think for himself. She wanted to be a drifter; he wanted a permanent home. She wanted to homeschool; he wanted to attend public schools. She wanted to eat all organic; he loved fast food. Whatever the issue, they tended to stand on opposite sides. They even had completely contrasting looks—her pale skin and light hair were nothing like the dark eyes and hair he'd inherited from his father.

However, he suspected the current downward turn of her lips wasn't about this particular disagreement. She was struggling to keep the infant in her arms from breaking into an all-out tantrum.

He almost felt guilty for piling this on her, but she'd brought on this lecture by meddling in his business. Again.

"Listen," she said, "Jessica has really been focused on the fact that she doesn't have a mother. I think she needs to have someone in her life to fill that role, even if it isn't someone you are involved with. She's eleven now. The last person she wants to talk to about preteen girl things is her dad. I've been there, Phil. I know how hard it is to be a single parent, especially to a child of the opposite sex. You can't fully understand what Jess is going through as she grows up. She needs someone to talk to."

Damn her for playing that card. He hated when she did that. Yes, he did know what it was like to grow up without one of his parents. Yes, he had blamed his mother for as long as he could remember. Yes, without a doubt, his daughter would benefit from having a woman in her life to turn to.

"She has you, Mom. Why the hell do you think I kept you around all those years?" He curved his lip into a half smile so she'd know he was teasing...but only a little. They'd never voiced the truth to each other, but he suspected they both understood Jessica was the tie that kept them bound together once he was old enough to be on his own.

If he hadn't needed his mother to help raise his daughter, they likely would have gone their own ways, seeing each other only when Kara made the effort to cross his path. Having Jessica had kept them in the same orbit. Having Harry, the only person who seemed to keep Kara grounded, back in their lives had set them on the path of mending their tattered relationship.

He wouldn't say he had completely let go of his resentment at being forced into her bohemian lifestyle, but at least he was working on it now. Settling down in his parents' hometown of Stonehill had brought the first real sense of belonging to Phil's heart. Though the small Midwestern town was a far cry from the West Coast where he'd spent all his life, Phil had adjusted. *Happily* adjusted. He had his father now. And his mother, whom he could finally see in a light that wasn't tainted with pure bitterness—just occasional hints of residual resentment.

"I will always be here for her," Kara said. "But having a grandma isn't the same as having a woman she can view as a mother figure. She's getting to be old enough to realize that."

"So I should just go grab the first woman I find and ask her to marry me and raise my kid?"

"That's not what she's saying," Harry stated. "Your mother has a genuine concern, Phil. Hear her out."

"It's been hard watching you spend your entire life focused only on raising Jess," Kara said. "You need more than just being a father to her to be truly happy. Trust me, sweetheart, I did the exact same thing you're doing. The big difference is that you're raising her without any of the fun stuff. At least I took you on adventures, taught you things you couldn't learn in school. We saw things, Phil. We went places."

This was their same old debate: her vagabond ways versus his desire for normalcy. "What's wrong with being close to family? It's actually nice, don't you think? To have a *real* home."

"Yes, Phil. It is nice. But there is more to life than just stability. Jess deserves to have fun. To experience things. So do you." She nodded toward her husband. "I think you'd be surprised how nice it is to have someone to share those things with. I know I was."

Once again, Phil inhaled deeply and let his breath out slowly. His mother had always had a way of trying his patience. She never knew when to quit. "Point taken. Now, changing the subject. Are you sure you don't want to come to lunch with Jess and me?"

"Not a chance," Harry said. "That little one will be taking a nap soon, and I'm making damn sure your mother and I follow suit."

"She was up all night again," Kara explained. "Your father is exhausted."

"So are you." Harry eyed her, and for a moment, Phil felt an odd sensation roll through him. Not jealousy exactly, but maybe the first real understanding of what his mom was saying. She'd never had anyone she could count on until she and Harry got back together. She'd always been on her own. She had friends—lovers too, he was sure—but she'd never had anyone who looked at her the way Harry did, like she was some wonderful thing to be cherished. Having someone to look at like that, and who looked at him like that in return, wouldn't be so bad.

Frowning at the droopy-eyed baby—and the idea that his

mother could be right—Phil asked, "When are you going to realize you've gotten suckered into raising this child?"

"We already have," Kara said. "But what would you have us do? Turn her out? Lynn can come and go to her heart's content, so long as we know this one is safe." She patted the baby's back and got a muted coo in return.

When Kara smiled contentedly, Phil pushed himself up. She'd never turn anyone out, not even a young mother who took advantage of her at every turn. While he'd made it his life's mission to find the stability he'd never had growing up, his mother's mission was to offer support that she'd been denied by her own family to frightened young mothers.

He knew how this was going to end, and his soul already ached for his parents. "It's going to break your heart when she takes Mira and leaves. And you know she'll leave sometime, Mom."

Kara cradled the baby a little closer. "Until then, Mira is going to know what it means to be cared for."

The image reminded Phil that one of the broken families his mother had cared for was his. His wife had left when Jessica was six months old. As soon as they'd found out the baby she was carrying had Down syndrome, she'd stopped wanting to have their daughter. Phil had convinced her not to end the pregnancy, but the medical conditions they'd faced after Jessica was born were too much for Katrina to handle. When the doctors said Jess had to have life-saving heart surgery, Katrina walked out the door and never looked back. Phil's mother had immediately stepped in to help him shoulder the emotional and financial burdens of Jessica's medical needs.

She'd held Jessica the same way she was holding little Mira, rocking gently, patting slowly, brushing her cheek over the baby's head. He'd harbored a lot of anger at his mother over the years, blaming her for his not having a father, but he could never be angry at her for caring about Jessica's needs. She'd always put Jess above everyone else, and even if she were butting in on his personal life, her motivation was the same as it had been since the day Jessica was born—she wanted to do what she perceived was best for her beloved granddaughter.

His anger softened, the edge dulled, as he watched the unbridled love radiating from his mother's soul. She was going to be inconsolable when this baby was taken from her. Her need to fix everything for everyone was admirable, but he wished she'd figure out how to quit while she was ahead. With Mira's mother *and* with him.

"Look, I know Jess needs someone in her life, but I'm not going to let just anyone in. She gets attached to people. She opens her heart to them, like you do. I don't want her to get hurt if that someone doesn't feel the same about her."

"I know." Kara looked up at him. "I'm just pointing out what I see, Phil. There's a void in that child's life. The same void you felt growing up. Sorry, Harry." She glanced at her husband, who dismissed her apology with a wave of his hand. "You know how it feels to not have someone in your life to connect with on that level. Jessica will always have me, but it isn't the same. You know that."

"Yes, I know." Phil kissed her head. "The baby's out."

"Hallelujah." Harry threw his hands up.

Bouncing into the room as if she were a kangaroo, Jessica yelled, "Daddy, I'm starving! Let's go!"

At Jess's loud, happy voice, Mira jolted and let out a wail. Phil chuckled as Harry dropped his hands with a miserable-sounding groan.

Mallory O'Connell eased open the front door of her mother's home and poked her head inside. She bit her lips to stop the giggle that threatened to erupt. She hadn't told her mom she was coming home from California. She'd wanted her arrival to be a surprise and couldn't wait to see the shock on her mother's face.

The last year had been difficult for the entire O'Connell family. Her mother had become a bit of a local celebrity, but not in a good way. Annie had been shot during a robbery gone wrong. The event shined a light on the increasing crime rate in their suburban community. Stonehill had always somehow seemed immune to those kinds of dangers. Even though Annie had survived, her ordeal made people more aware. Neighbors glanced over their shoulders and hugged their purses a bit more closely as they walked around the town square.

Annie's recovery had been slow, but her family was

determined to return to normal because, as they all insisted, life went on. Annie had finally married Marcus Callison, the man who had been by her side long before she'd actually needed a shoulder to lean on. Mallory had graduated from college and accepted her dream job. But that job had taken her to San Diego —far away from Stonehill, her family, and Annie's recovery.

Mallory loved her work, loved the city, but being away from her mom had taken its toll. Just four months after moving to California, Mallory decided to return to the Midwest. She was the epitome of independence—Annie had raised her that way— but she'd damn near lost her mother. Her budding career and big dreams didn't seem so important anymore. Traveling the world moved down on her to-do list. Being independent didn't have quite the same meaning as it had when she'd been a teenager eager to leave home. Her priorities had changed; she just hadn't realized that until she was gone.

Months had passed since she'd simply sat down next to Annie and had a conversation. She wanted that more than anything—more than was probably logical for a grown woman, but that didn't make her want it any less. She needed to be home to see her mom through her recovery and spend as much time with her family as possible. That was what had become the most important thing to her.

Easing the door closed behind her, Mallory listened for signs of life in the house. She heard the television and pictured Marcus enthralled with some old movie while Annie sat on the other end of the couch with her nose stuck in a book.

After quietly dropping her bags by the door, Mallory tiptoed toward the living room, a childish excitement filling her and making her heart beat faster. When she was about eight, she'd discovered how easy it was to sneak up and startle her mom. She'd done it over and over—easing into the kitchen and screaming *boo!* just to make her mom squeal. She hadn't stopped until her mother suffered a severe brain trauma and scaring her seemed more cruel than funny.

However, this time was different. This time she wasn't scaring them for a laugh. This was like the best kind of surprise. She couldn't wait to see their faces when she popped around the corner. Her mom was going to freak—in a good way. However, when she bounced into the living room, a big smile on her face, she was the only one taken aback. Annie was straddling Marcus's lap, her blouse hanging off her shoulders. Marcus kissed her neck and cupped her...

Gross!

Mallory covered her eyes and turned her back on her parental units as she gasped loudly. "Seriously? Are you guys sixteen?"

"Mallory?" Annie asked. Though the residual effects of her injury made her voice a bit slurred, she sounded just as shocked as her daughter. "What are you doing here?"

"Getting scarred for life, apparently. What are you *doing?*" She pressed her palms to her ears. "No. Don't answer that. Do *not* answer that." Dropping her hands, she glanced at her parents and winced. "I'm going to go get lunch. You guys finish..." She shuddered at the thought, which she immediately banished. "Oh, gross. This is just...*ick*! I'll be back later."

"Wait," Annie called.

By the time Annie caught up to Mallory, she'd pressed the Velcro fasteners on her blouse closed. Kara Martinson-Canton had adapted all of Annie's clothes so she'd feel more independent during the months she was regaining the use of her hands. Mal felt all icky inside when she realized easy-on also meant her mother's clothes were easy to remove. Annie's straight blond hair was a ruffled mess, and her lips were pink and puffy. Mallory looked away from the whisker burn on her mother's neck and cringed at the image that would forever be embedded in her mind.

"Mom. Really. I'm going to run to the café. When I come back, we can try this happy homecoming thing again. With less...nudity. A *lot* less nudity."

Annie shook her head and put her hands to Mallory's shoulders to stop her from moving away. "What are you doing here?"

The brain injury was more than enough reason as far as Mal was concerned. Her mother's voice used to be so clear and commanding. Now every word had to be painstakingly enunciated, drawing attention to how much she still struggled. Even if Annie was actively recovering, hearing her mother speak on the phone, listening to Annie's continued battles toward recovery, made Mallory's heart break. Not being in Stonehill with her mom was killing her a little each day.

Marcus stepped around Mallory and stood next to his wife. "Are you okay, Mal?"

She frowned. "I just witnessed my parents making out on the sofa like unsupervised teenagers. No. I'm not okay. I'm permanently damaged." Heat rose to her cheeks, and she had no doubt her skin was as red as Annie's.

"Is something wrong?" he pressed. "Did something happen?"

Mallory forced a smile. "Nope. Just missed you guys."

Suspicion clouded Annie's eyes. Her mother might have lost some abilities after being injured, but seeing right through Mallory wasn't one.

"I'm going to the café."

"Don't leave," Marcus said.

Mallory scrunched up her face. "No. Really. I need to bleach my eyes. And I'm starving. I just hope I can keep down whatever I eat." She pushed her way between them, snatched her purse from her pile of bags, and was out the door in seconds. She drew a deep breath, inhaling the crisp early spring air, concentrating on the sharpness in her lungs.

While seeing her mom on the verge of having sex was something she definitely could have lived her entire life without experiencing, Mallory had to chuckle. At least some aspects of her mother's recovery were on track.

That gross feeling washed over her again. She shook her head hard, trying to dislodge the image. The only way to fix this was a hot meal and hotter coffee.

CHAPTER TWO

*M*allory parked in front of the Stonehill Café and rushed toward the door. Though the sun was shining, the air was still bitter from a long winter and the breeze sweeping down Main Street went straight through Mallory's sweatshirt and into her bones. The bell above the café door chimed as she hurried inside. She glanced around for a moment before her heart swelled and a smile broke across her face.

Her stepdad's sister, Jenna, owner of the café, gasped when she noticed Mal walking in the door. Though the old building needed massive upgrades, Jenna was an amazing cook and today seemed to be taking on the role of both cook and waitress. Though she had a dusting of flour on her Bee Gees T-shirt, she was also seating a couple at a booth. She dropped two menus and said she'd be right back then made a beeline for Mallory. The dark brown bun on the top of her head bounced with every step as she spread her arms wide in anticipation of a big hug.

"Oh my God," Jenna gushed. "If it isn't my favorite niece, back from California."

"I'm your only niece." Mallory embraced the woman who had really only been her aunt for the four months since Annie and Marcus had married.

Jenna was a nurturer and had made Mallory feel like she'd been a part of their family long before she really was. Just as Mallory had started treating Marcus like a father before he and Annie had even started dating. In a way, Jenna had been her aunt even before her mom and Jenna's brother had married.

Breaking the embrace, Jenna put her hand to Mallory's cheek and peered into her eyes as if assessing the wellness of her soul. "I didn't know you were in town."

"I wanted to surprise Mom."

"Aw, honey, I bet she's over the moon."

Mallory laughed. "Yeah. She's...something." Curiosity touched Jenna's eyes, but Mal didn't expand on her comment. "I'm starving and in desperate need of sustenance. I've been on the road for the last two days. I need real food and strong coffee."

"Well, you came to the right place. Take a seat, sweetie. I'll bring you a cup in just a sec."

Mallory was sliding into a booth by the window when she noticed a little girl peeking over the top of the cracked red vinyl seat across from her. She grinned, immediately recognizing her. "Hey, Jessica."

The girl beamed, clearly thrilled that Mal remembered her.

"What's up?" Mallory asked.

"The sky."

Mallory laughed more than the joke required. "Very clever. How are you?"

Jessica rested her folded arms on the back of the booth and her smile widened. "Jenna added rainbow pancakes to the menu. And guess what?"

Mal didn't have a chance to guess before Jessica told her.

"She named them after me because she didn't have rainbow pancakes until *I* asked her to make them. They are on the kid section, but she'll let you order them. You should. They are *delicious*."

"I bet they are." Mallory couldn't help but feel excited for the girl. Clearly this was a big accomplishment for her. Then again, who didn't want pancakes named after them?

A few beats passed as Jessica narrowed her eyes thoughtfully. "I thought you moved away."

"I did. But I came home to see my mom."

"I don't have a mom," she said as casually as one might comment on the weather.

Mallory opened her mouth but wasn't quite sure how to respond. She knew that Jessica's mother had bailed when the girl was an infant. Mal understood the hole in Jessica's life—her dad had ducked out before she was even born. Annie had been a single mother from the moment she'd told him she was pregnant.

"I didn't have a dad for a long time," Mallory said, wanting to give the girl hope, "but then my mom got married. To Jenna's brother, actually. I like to think of him as my dad, even though he really isn't. And that makes Jenna my aunt."

Jessica rolled her eyes with all the disgust the rainbow-pancake-loving little girl seemed to be able to muster. "My dad will *never* get married. He's too peculiar."

Mallory didn't mean to laugh, but the sound ripped from her chest. She'd met Jessica's father. He was cute. Nice. A bit of a hippie, but he *was* Kara's child, and that woman looked like she'd walked out of a Woodstock documentary. Even so, Phil hadn't seemed odd to Mallory. "What do you mean, he's too peculiar?"

"Grandma says that he'll never find a girlfriend if he doesn't stop being so picky."

"Oh. You mean *particular*."

Jess shrugged, as if she didn't care that she'd used the wrong word. "Grandma says it's important that Daddy be choosy, but he can't expect to find someone if he never dates anyone. He says he'll date when he's ready, but I think he is ready, because I caught him flirting with my teacher." Jessica looked up and smiled when a throat cleared as someone approached her table. "Hi, Daddy."

Phil seemed to have overheard at least a part of the conversation he'd interrupted. He had an air of disapproval on his face as he drew his mouth tight and lifted his brows at his daughter. "Hey, Punk."

"Did you remember to use a paper towel to open the bathroom door so you don't get germs on your fingers?"

He nodded. "I did. Thanks for checking."

Jessica returned her attention to Mallory. "Some people don't wash their hands after using the bathroom, so you should always use a paper towel or your sleeve to open the bathroom door."

"Good tip. Thanks." Mallory tried to hide her smile but figured her amusement was out there for the world to see. Jessica's father, on the other hand, still didn't appear amused. "Hi, Phil. How are you?" Mallory asked to rescue the girl from his scowl.

He stared, as if not quite sure who she was. Most people who knew Annie immediately recognized Mal as the woman's offspring. From her straight blond hair to her pointed nose and cool gray eyes, Mallory was practically identical to her mother.

"Mallory O'Connell. We met at my uncle Paul's wedding. I'm Annie's daughter."

Recognition lit his eyes as he nodded. "Right. How's your mom?"

"She's okay. Getting better every day, so she says."

"I was glad the guy pled so Annie didn't have to go through the trial. My mom said she was really worried about having to testify."

Yet another reason why Mallory had hated being away from home. Anticipating the trial had been nerve-racking for Annie and Marcus. Neither had wanted to relive the moment their lives had changed forever. They hadn't said as much to her, though.

Mallory heard from her uncles how choked up Annie still got talking about the moment a bullet ripped through her and how she didn't seem willing to do that in front of the man who had hurt her. Her mother had reluctantly given a statement at the sentencing hearing and only because the prosecution insisted the judge needed to see firsthand how much damage had been done. Mallory knew that alone would have been stressful and was glad Annie hadn't had to sit on the stand and answer detailed questions about the incident and her recovery.

Phil put his hands casually into his pockets. "I thought you were—"

"In California," she finished. "Yes. I was. I just got back, actually."

"For good or just visiting?"

"For good. I felt like a shi—" Her gaze darted to where Jessica was still peering over the booth, hanging on her every word. "Like a jerk not being here for Mom. I know she and Marcus can use my help right now. Even if they won't admit it."

He furrowed his thick brows as concern filled his dark eyes. Though Kara clearly impacted his taste in attire, his olive skin and dark features were all Harry Canton. "Is she really okay?"

"She doesn't like when people feel sorry for her," Jessica said. "If you feel sorry for her, she's going to be mad at you."

Jessica wasn't wrong. Annie and Marcus both would be furious if they knew the real reason Mallory had given up her dream job and living in SoCal was that she felt so damned guilty living her own life that she couldn't even sleep at night.

While Annie had been in the hospital recovering, she and Jessica bonded over their disabilities. Jessica had grown up dealing with pity, but that kind of attention was new to Annie, and she hadn't handled it well. Kara had made an effort to bring Jessica around once she saw Annie interacting with the girl. Kara said one of Jessica's natural talents was helping people who didn't know they needed it. She was right. Without even being aware of what she was doing, Jessica was able to guide Annie to the inner strength she needed to stop being angry about her situation and to start recovering. The two had forged a strong bond, one that was evident in Jessica's defense of Annie now.

"I'm not feeling sorry for her," Mal said. "I just want to be here for her."

Phil gestured to the table that Jessica hadn't faced since Mallory sat down. "Finish your pancakes, Punk."

Jessica huffed but turned and disappeared behind the booth.

Phil sank into the seat across from Mallory. The concern in his brown eyes was almost enough to make Mallory cry, though she didn't understand why. She wasn't the one who needed the help. She was the one who had come home to help.

"I know worrying and family go hand in hand," Phil said, "but your mom really does seem to be doing okay. She and Marcus came to Jessica's birthday party last weekend. She smiled and laughed and seemed to enjoy herself. Marcus had to help her a little bit, sure, but she really was okay."

"Good to hear."

Jenna set a cup of coffee in front of Mallory and smiled at the little face poking over the seat. "How are your pancakes, Miss Jess?"

"Fine," Jessica said with a pout to her voice.

Mallory tried not to chuckle, but a giggle escaped. "Can I get some of those rainbow pancakes she was telling me about?" she asked to atone for the slip.

"The Jessica Special? Coming right up. Phil, you need anything?" She glanced between the two adults, clearly trying to gauge what was going on.

"No, thanks, Jen. I'm good." Phil waited for Jenna to disappear before looking at Mallory again. "You didn't answer me before—and feel free to tell me it's none of my business—but is Annie okay?"

"Yeah, she's fine. I mean, she's not *fine*, she's...got residual issues, but..." She laughed awkwardly. "She's not in a coma anymore, right?" Her smile faded, and she sipped her coffee as he scrutinized her from across the table. Finally she set the cup down and fell back in the booth. "Sorry. I tend to make inappropriate jokes when I'm upset."

"I don't mean to upset you."

She frowned as he gave her an encouraging smile. His mother had that same look. The one that made the words want to pour out of Mallory. When Annie was in the hospital and no one knew if she'd live, let alone recover, Kara had a way about her that made Mallory want to break down and let out some of her fear. She never had. She'd been too terrified that the reality of her mother's condition would consume her. That fear still lingered in the back of her mind.

Even though Annie was on the road to recovery, she'd never be the same. Nothing would ever be the same. That was terrifying. Mallory had never let the horror of what she felt really touch her. She attributed that trait to Annie. The woman was stronger than granite. But even granite cracked sometimes, and the way Phil was looking at her now made Mallory want to crumble. He apparently practiced the same emotional voodoo as his mother.

Mallory took a deep breath to brace herself against his dark powers. "Mom's probably handling her disabilities better than I am," she confessed. "No. She's definitely handling her disabilities better than I am. She was always the strongest person I knew, completely unshakable. Seeing her... God, I sound like an ass."

"No, you don't," Phil reassured her. "You sound like someone who is struggling with a drastically changed reality. Maybe I should be asking if you're okay."

"I felt guilty not being here." She stared at him hard. "And if you *ever* repeat that, I will deny it to my dying breath."

He crossed his heart. "Your secret's safe with me."

"I stayed in California as long as I could. I wanted to come home so many times."

"What was the final push?"

"Uncle Paul slipped. He said she was having a hard time coping with this brick wall she's hit in her recovery. The therapist doesn't think her speech will get any better, and regaining full use of her hands is taking longer than they thought. She's struggling with that. I realized it was time. I need to be here. I need to help her, even if she doesn't want me to."

"I don't think that's the issue, Mallory. Of course she wants you home and close. She talked about you so much at Jessica's party. She's incredibly proud of you. I think she just wants you to be happy and worries that taking time out of your life to care for her isn't going to make you happy. My unsolicited advice would be that since you've made the decision to come home, make a point to have a life outside of looking after Annie. Or you'll both regret your decision."

Phil gave her that damned comforting smile again. He had a little dimple in his left cheek that drew her attention until she forced her focus back to her coffee cup. She'd talked to her family and friends about this, but something about the understanding in Phil's eyes made her feel that coming home simply because she needed to be closer to Annie didn't make her a baby. She appreciated that more than he could ever know, and apparently more than she could say, since she couldn't seem to find the words to thank him for being sympathetic. Or figure out why all of a sudden her eyes burned with unshed tears.

"Sorry," she whispered, snagging a napkin from the dispenser on the table.

"Parents can be a handful, huh?" he asked softly.

She laughed quietly as she dabbed her tears before they could fall. "Sometimes."

"Speaking of which"—he indicated the booth behind him

with a jerk of his head—"I wasn't flirting with her teacher. Just so you know."

"Yes, you were," Jessica called.

He rolled his eyes and shook his head. Mallory chuckled, but her amusement didn't last. Annie and Marcus, both looking worried, approached the table.

Mallory sarcastically cocked a brow at her mom and stepdad. "Finished already?"

Annie frowned then looked at Phil. "Is Jess here?"

Jessica peeked over the booth again. "Hey, Annie."

Annie's face lit with a bright smile. She clearly had a genuine affection for the little girl. "Hi, honey. How are you?"

"Mallory's going to eat some of my pancakes," she stated matter-of-factly, as if that answered the question.

"Well, she won't be disappointed."

"That's what I told her. I also told her not to, but she feels sorry for you," Jess offered.

"All right, Punk." Phil slid out of his booth and dug into his pocket. "Time to go."

"But—"

He dropped some cash on the table. "But nothing. Let's go. Nice to see you guys," he said to Annie and Marcus before turning to Mallory. He mouthed *sorry*, and she shrugged in return.

As Phil dragged Jessica away, despite her insistence that she wasn't done with her pancakes, Annie slid into the booth next to Mallory.

"It wasn't working," Mal said before her mother could ask. "That's all. California wasn't working."

Annie wrapped her arm around Mallory's shoulders and tilted her face down, clearly analyzing her daughter. "How so?"

"I...I missed being here. I wanted to come home. I thought you'd be thrilled."

"I am. But are you?"

Mallory looked at Marcus as he took the seat Phil had vacated. His face had the same questions as Annie's mixed with the sympathy that Phil had shown her. Clearly she wasn't covering her motives for coming home as well as she thought.

"I missed you guys, okay?" she asked. "I know that makes me sound pathetic, but I wanted to be closer to you. *All* of you. Uncles, aunts, cousins. Even my overbearing mother." She hoped her teasing jab would break the tension at the table, but her joke fell flat. Annie didn't smile or take the bait or offer up her own dry retort. She just stared with that same air of concern. "Mom, I hated being away from my family. I thought I would love the independence, but I didn't. I wanted to come home."

Annie and Marcus cast doubtful glances, but it was Annie who spoke. "Because of me?"

"Because I *missed* you."

Marcus put his hands on Mallory's. "How long are you home for?"

"Permanently," she said, hating the sound of that word. "I quit my job and paid out my lease."

"Why?" Marcus knitted his brows together, but she couldn't

determine if it was frustration, concern, confusion, or all of the above. He'd been the one who had helped her negotiate the terms of her lease. Next to Annie, Marcus was the best real estate agent Mallory knew. He'd fought tooth and nail to get a sweet deal that she'd blown.

"I wanted to come home," she stated. "End of story."

Annie lowered her face for a moment before looking at Mallory again. There was something in her eyes—pain, maybe even a hint of embarrassment. "So it is because of me."

Guilt settled in Mallory's stomach. She had hoped coming home would make her parents happy. Suddenly her decision seemed to pile on to their mountain of problems. She wasn't lying, though. Sure, part of it was because she felt as if she were ducking out on her responsibilities—driving her mom to appointments and helping with her therapy shouldn't fall solely on Marcus—but she truly had missed her family. "No, Mom," she said with determination. "I came home because I want be *here*. San Diego is great. I really liked living there, but my family is *here*."

Marcus gave Mallory a smile that didn't look the least bit sincere. He was visibly trying to hide his concerns in front of Annie. Mallory suspected the first time he could get her alone, he'd have one of those fatherly conversations he'd mastered while Annie had been in a coma after the shooting. He really had become a dad to Mallory—but this was one instance when she'd rather he hadn't. He was going to push and push until he got the answers he wanted from her.

"Hey," he said through that fake smile, "it'll be great to have you home. We've missed you, too. Haven't we, honey?"

Annie frowned but nodded. "Yeah. We have."

Jenna slid a plate of pancakes in front of Mallory, eyeing her brother as she did. The plate skidded to a stop, and the pile of half-melted whipped cream oozed off the colorful stack as sprinkles melted into puddles of various hues.

Mallory sank back as disappointment settled in her stomach. Nothing about her surprise homecoming had turned out the way she'd planned.

sh

Phil handed Harry a purple, unicorn-shaped overnight bag as his daughter ran through his parents' house, straight for the kitchen, where Kara was preparing dinner. "Are you sure about this?"

Despite the frown on his face and the dark circles under his eyes, Harry nodded and accepted the offering. "Kara is worried she's not getting enough attention."

"Well. She does have a doting father."

Dropping the bag at the foot of the stairs, Harry didn't seem to have the strength to be apologetic for the offense Phil took at the statement. "From her grandparents. Mira is taking up a lot of our time these days."

"You don't say."

Harry leaned against the railing as if he couldn't stand on his own much longer. "Kara can't put her down long enough to rest when she's here, and she can't stop worrying long enough to rest when she's gone."

Phil's concern spiked. He'd noticed his parents were spread thin with the infant, but this was the first time Harry had expressed frustration. "Dad, this is too much."

His frown deepened. "We know. Trust me, we know. She showed up here drunk last night, insisting on taking the baby. She said she is moving in with some guy we've never even heard of. Apparently they want to be a family. Kara took her sweet time getting Mira's things together until Lynn passed out on the couch. She was gone when we woke up this morning, but damned if either of us slept a wink. We were too terrified she'd sneak out with the baby and wrap them both around a telephone pole."

"You have to turn her in, Dad."

"We talked to someone this morning. But she's the kid's mother. Until she actually does put Mira in danger—"

"Or gets her killed," Phil snapped.

"Or gets her killed," Harry said with defeat, "there isn't anything we can do but try to protect her as much as Lynn will allow."

Phil swallowed, guilt filling his gut like a bag of wet cement. He'd been giving his mom such a hard time for putting her heart on the line for Mira when clearly they were doing more than just babysitting—they were trying to protect her from real harm. "I didn't realize it was that bad."

"Your mom—"

"Didn't want me to worry," Phil finished.

Harry let the topic fall when Kara walked into the room, her long hair in that same haphazard bun as she expertly wrapped Mira against her chest with the long strip of cloth she used to keep the infant secure against her but which allowed her hands to be free.

"Are you hungry? I just put a chicken pot pie in the oven." Though she looked exhausted, she offered him a smile that he thought he'd probably been taking for granted most of his life.

When he was a kid, moving from place to place on her whim, he'd always thought she was too self-centered to care that he wanted to plant roots and have a real home where he could belong. He'd deliberately been a brat to her most of his life. Only after Harry found Kara in Seattle, quite by accident, did Phil learn the truth about his mother's lifelong heartache and the real reason she found it so hard to stay in one place too long. Whenever she stopped moving, the pain she felt at the rejection of being turned out when she'd gotten pregnant as a teen would catch up to her. Constantly starting over was her way of never having to face the hurt.

He'd never even seen what she was going through. She'd hidden it so well. Or he'd been so focused on himself that he'd never bothered to see. Either way, he saw it now. He saw through the fake smile and exhausted eyes. The situation with Mira was more than just some young girl taking advantage of two kind people. Kara and Harry were the only ones preventing something truly terrible from happening to the baby, and that was taking a toll on his mother.

As he held her bloodshot gaze, he thought of Mallory and the haunted look he'd seen in her eyes earlier in the day. She'd come so close to losing Annie that the fear still seemed to have a grip on her. Looking at the woman whom he had only recently come to really know and understand, fear touched his own heart. He couldn't imagine what he and Jess would do without his mother. If something happened to her like what had happened to Annie, he would probably look as scared and unsettled as Mallory had when she spoke of her mom's slow recovery.

Kara had cared for him all his life and had stepped in to care for Jessica just as easily and wholeheartedly as she was stepping in to take care of Mira. Yeah, he'd definitely taken that smile of hers for granted.

"Dinner would be great," he said. "Thanks, Mom."

Her smile widened. She seemed genuinely pleased that he was sticking around instead of just dropping Jessica off and running.

"Why don't you guys sit for a while," he said. "Jess and I can finish up dinner."

"I'd love to," Kara said, "but if I stop moving, she starts screaming."

"I'll take her."

She started to argue, but Phil crossed the entryway and pulled Mira away. Kara seemed to hold her breath waiting, but when Mira didn't start wailing, she helped Phil wrap the baby against his chest. Though he hadn't held an infant for some time, he wasn't exactly out of practice. Kara was a midwife, and plenty of babies had come in and out of their lives. He was more on the "fun uncle" level of practice these days, but that would be enough to give his parents a break.

With Mira content against him, he headed into the kitchen. "Nice job, Punk," he said, regarding the table Jessica was setting. "Make a spot for me."

She jumped up and down then stopped and stared at the lump against him. "Mira let you hold her?"

He cupped his fingers around his lips and whispered like he was relaying some great secret. "I don't think she knows yet."

Jess put her hand to her mouth and giggled. "Just wait till she figures it out. She's gonna blow a basket."

"Gasket," he corrected as he grabbed a washrag to clean the flour and little balls of homemade dough from the counter. "I have a plan to surprise Grandma and Grandpa. Think you can help me?"

There was nothing Jessica liked more than being included in secrets and surprises. "What's your plan?"

"Grandma and Grandpa are trying so hard to help Mira that I think we should help them. Can you go get all the dirty laundry and bring it downstairs so we can wash it?"

"Grandma doesn't like how you do laundry, Daddy," she said, her tone dire and full of warning.

"Grandma doesn't like how I do anything, but since we're helping her, she'll be happy." He offered her a wink. "Trust me."

"*Okay.*" She drew out the word as she pushed herself from the counter. "But don't say I didn't warn you."

He watched her dart from the room and then went to work on cleaning up the kitchen. He didn't stop with wiping the counter and loading the dishwasher like he usually did when he stayed for dinner at his parents' house. This time, however, he hummed and bounced to soothe the baby as he gathered the trash from various cans downstairs, took the overflowing bag to the bin outside, and filled the mop bucket. Mira remained content enough through the process, even babbling a few times, as if to tell him she approved.

With the laundry gathered, Phil showed Jessica how to sort into piles and then gave the floors a quick cleaning. By the time he finished, Jessica had put a load in, and he did a quick glance before offering her a high five. While he added detergent, she took the glass cleaner to give the bathroom a quick scrub. When the timer on the oven dinged, Phil rushed to save his mother's dinner. Convinced the pie needed a few more minutes, he headed to the living room to tell his parents to wash up. A kind of childish excitement made him smile, eager to see the happiness and surprise on his mom's face when she saw the much-improved state of her home.

"Hey..." His words trailed off and his smile fell when he stepped into the room.

Harry was on the sofa, his head back as he inhaled a deep, vibrating breath. Kara's head was on his lap, one of his hands buried in her hair, the other resting on her stomach as she lay with her mouth open, sleeping just as deeply but not nearly as loudly.

The image tugged at something Phil couldn't quite pin down. A chord, one he hadn't known was tied to his heart, was struck, and he felt something akin to...loneliness.

He'd had a few casual relationships since his wife left, but his focus had always been on his daughter. Some women were hesitant to get close to him, knowing Jessica's special needs might require more of his attention than most kids would otherwise need. Some women seemed so in awe of him for being a single dad to a child with Down syndrome that he felt more like a pet project than a boyfriend. He had yet to find someone he felt confident would be there for him and Jess for the right reasons and for the long haul. He'd been fine with casual, though. Casual meant nobody got hurt.

Even after he was an adult and a father, he always felt that he had his hands full with his mom. Besides raising Jessica, he had a hell of a time keeping Kara on the right track—she had been like a wayward teen most of his life. He hadn't been able to focus solely on himself and his daughter until Harry came back into their lives and filled the void Kara had seemed unable to fill in his life. Now, Jess was growing up and testing out her independence as much as any eleven-year-old could. She needed more than Phil and Kara and Harry could give her, and for some reason he couldn't explain, Phil suddenly felt like he might need more too.

He wanted his parents to be happy. He was thrilled they were happy, but seeing them so tightly bonded made him feel alone in a way that adult children shouldn't feel left out by their parents' closeness.

"Daddy," Jess called.

He turned and put his finger to his lips, warning her to quiet down.

"I'm done in the bathroom," she whispered. "Want me to do the bathroom upstairs?"

"That'd be great, Punk. Thanks. Then wash up and come right back down. I'll serve us some dinner."

She rushed off, clearly happy to have a chore to do. He looked back at his sleeping parents, patted the baby's back, and headed to the kitchen, determined to shake the hollow feeling that had suddenly found its way low in his gut.

CHAPTER THREE

*M*allory went straight for Phil and Jessica. The father-daughter duo sat in the same booth she always found them in at Stonehill Café. She didn't wait for an invite. She slid in next to Jessica and playfully bumped into her. "Fancy meeting you here."

"We always eat here on Sunday morning," Jessica announced. "It's tradition. That's how I got pancakes named after me."

Phil didn't counter the girl's logic. "Pancakes that you never finish."

Jessica ignored him. "You should order them. They're rainbow."

Mal smiled, not pointing out that she already knew that. "Very cool." Turning to Phil, she kept her grin plastered to her face. "And very filling, Dad."

He glanced around, as if expecting to see someone. "Are you here alone? Where're your mom and Marcus?"

"They were still holed up in their room when I left."

"Really? Aren't our elders usually out and about by this hour?"

She scrunched up her face as she flashed back to the week before when she'd arrived unexpectedly. "After surprising them last Saturday morning, I don't want to know how they spend their time."

Phil chuckled. "And I don't want to know what that means."

She widened her eyes dramatically. "No, you don't. Let's just say the lesson came a little late in life, but I've finally learned to knock before entering a room."

"Well, if you recall, my parents haven't been married all that long. I learned that lesson the hard way as well."

"Grownups are nasty," she whispered. She smiled up at her aunt Jenna when a coffee mug was set in front of her. "Morning, Jen."

"Where're your parents?"

Instead of rehashing her fears, Mallory settled on telling her they were still sleeping. Jenna put a menu in front of her, but Mallory waved it off.

"Oh, I was just stopping to say hi. I'm not crashing their breakfast."

"Stay," Phil insisted. "We like the company, don't we, Punk?"

Jessica nodded as she shoved whipped cream and sprinkle-covered pancakes into her mouth. Mallory conceded with a nod and ordered a plate of the Jessica Special with a side of bacon.

The girl next to her beamed with pride as she again told the story of how the pancakes came to be named.

Mallory tried to fight her smile as Phil reminded Jessica not to talk with her mouth full. When the girl was back to chewing, mouth closed, he cut into his own stack of pancakes. Mallory swiped back a few strands of Jessica's dark brown hair that stuck to her cheek, trapped by a splatter of whipped cream.

"How was your first week back?" Phil asked.

"Busy," Mallory said. "First thing I did was start looking at Mom's rental properties. Love her and Marcus to pieces, but I'm not staying with them now that I know what they do on the couch when I'm not looking."

Phil laughed. "Find anything?"

"Yeah, I did, actually." She sipped from her mug before announcing, "I am now the proud renter of a cute little two-bedroom piled high with boxes that I can't seem to find the energy to unpack. The whole of the O'Connell family has offered to help, but I refused. I don't want them sorting through my stuff. My uncles unloaded my furniture when the moving truck arrived yesterday. I got that out of the way, but the boxes will be dealt with on my terms."

"Hiding bodies?" he asked.

She shrugged. "That's my little secret."

"Hey." Jessica pointed out the window. "There's Grandma and Grandpa."

Mallory looked to where Jessica was waving. Kara had never been one to dress up, but she looked like a hot damn mess in a multicolored ankle-length skirt with a black T-shirt and her strawberry-blond hair in a messy braid, pinned back. Harry, in unusually disheveled and wrinkled clothes, opened the back door of his car and, a few moments later, pulled out a car seat.

Mallory couldn't stop her eyes from widening. "*Whoa.* Your parents had a baby? No wonder they look like hell." She gasped and put her fingers to her mouth. "I-I-I didn't mean that...like it sounded. I meant..."

Phil shook his head. "Don't apologize. You are absolutely correct. They look like hell. And they didn't *have* a baby. They've gotten stuck raising someone else's."

Jessica sighed theatrically. "Grandma always takes in strays."

The girl was clearly repeating something she'd heard—probably from Phil, since he winced noticeably.

"Uh." He cleared his throat. "Let's not say that anymore, huh, Punk? I don't think Grandma would see the humor in comparing babies to puppies." He met Mallory's gaze. "Mom has always helped single mothers get on their feet. This particular one, however, doesn't seem very interested in finding her own way. She all but disappeared after having the baby. My parents spend much more time with that kid than her birth mother does. Which is a good thing, really. Dad said the woman showed up drunk the other night and passed out on their couch."

Mallory frowned. She didn't think she had a maternal bone in her body, but even she knew that wasn't how the parenting thing was supposed to go. "How sad. Poor kid."

Phil sighed loudly. "At least she has my parents."

The café door opened, and the rest of the Martinson-Canton clan entered. Jessica nudged at Mallory, who slid out of the booth to let the girl slip by. Jessica darted across the café to hug her grandma. Kara kissed the top of her head, but she never took her gaze off the table—off Mallory and Phil. If Mallory didn't know better, she'd swear a conspiratorial grin passed between Phil's parents when Kara finally did break her intense stare long enough to glance at Harry.

"They really look exhausted," Mallory said in a horrified whisper.

"They are." Phil's answer was just as quiet. "That kid has a serious aversion to sleeping."

Her horror grew as she got a better look at Kara's pale skin and the bags under her bloodshot eyes. "Is that what having a baby does to you?"

"Yes," Phil answered. "Yes, it is. The life force drains from you for a good two years."

"No wonder I was an only child." She put on a wide smile when the Cantons continued staring at her. "Hey, you two—er —three..."

"Hey, Mallory," Kara practically sang as she walked hand in hand with Jessica to the table. "I heard you were back in town."

"Yeah. California just wasn't all it was cracked up to be."

Kara's eyes, tired as they were, softened. She took a breath and started to say something but then seemed to reconsider.

Mallory looked at Phil, who simply shrugged. Turning her

attention back to Kara, she lifted her brows. "Come on. Spit it out."

"Your mom is okay," she said with that same sweet tone that used to do Mal in after Annie had been shot. "She really is. She's as tough as ever on the inside."

Mallory nodded firmly. She'd never doubted her mother's drive. "I know."

"Marcus knows when to help and when to back off. When he doesn't, she tells him."

"I know."

"Don't worry about her, okay? That's her husband's job now."

"I know."

Kara scowled at her, but even the dark circles and deep frown didn't take the concern from her eyes. "Did you learn your communication skills from my son?"

Mallory smiled. "He taught me well."

Eyeing Phil, Kara smirked. "Well, then you two shouldn't have any problems talking in the future."

Harry grinned down at his son. "We didn't mean to interrupt your breakfast. Mira's actually in a decent mood this morning. We thought we'd try breakfast out for a change."

"Better eat before she changes her mind," Phil said.

"Yes," Harry said, pulling his wife away. "Yes, we should."

Kara kissed Jess again. "See you later, sweetheart."

Jess wasn't so willing to let her grandmother go, though. She clung to her hand and begged her father, "Can I sit with Grandma? *Please.*"

"Sure," Phil said.

Kara's smile widened as she held her other hand out for Jessica's plate. "Enjoy your breakfast, guys."

Phil sighed when he and Mallory were alone. "Oh, man. This isn't good."

"There was a whole lot of something going on there that I don't know about," Mallory agreed.

He lifted his coffee mug. "You don't want to know."

"But I have a feeling I *should* know." She sat back when Jenna slid a plate in front of her and then topped off her coffee. "What is it?" Mallory asked after her aunt left their table to seat Kara, Harry, and the kids.

Pushing his cup aside, Phil crossed his arms on the table and leaned close as he lowered his voice. "My parents are trying to marry me off. Congratulations. They've just added you to the pool of possibilities."

Mallory cocked a brow as his words sank in. Finally, she shrugged and gestured toward herself. "Look at this face. You could do worse."

Phil was about halfway through six months' worth of Mallory's social media photos when she messaged him asking what he was doing. She'd sent him a friend request sometime after breakfast that morning. As soon as he accepted, he did what was the social media norm.

Judging your life based on your social media photos, he replied.

Funny. I was doing the same about yours.

He smiled at the thought of her cyberstalking him too. *And?*

You have to get out more.

Phil laughed, mainly because he couldn't disagree. *I'm a single dad with sole custody of an eleven-year-old drama queen. I enjoy peace and quiet when I can get it. San Diego looked great. That's probably one of the only places along the West Coast we didn't live when I was growing up. Miss it?*

I'll say yes, but only if you promise not to tell anyone.

Promise. What are you up to? he asked, fearing she'd end the conversation on that note. *Besides judging my life.*

Staring at boxes, wishing they'd unpack themselves. You?

Phil looked around his empty living room. Jessica hadn't taken kindly to her sleepover the night before ending before it really began. After Phil had pulled the chicken pot pie from the oven, he and Jess had eaten while his parents continued their nap on the couch. He'd helped her get ready for bed, as much as she would allow, amid her protests that she was there to see her grandparents.

She never said as much, but Phil knew Jess wanted to be certain she was the front and center of Kara and Harry's attention, so she'd begged to spend the night again...this time without Grandma and Grandpa falling asleep on the couch.

Even though his parents looked like they could fall over at any moment and it was a school night, they'd agreed she could stay, giving Phil an evening of peace and quiet. For some reason, the quiet wasn't sitting well with him. He started to type, stopped, then started again.

Finally, he typed, *I was thinking about grabbing some beer and pizza and coming over to help you unpack.*

Beer and pizza, yes. Unpacking my stuff? No.

You really are hiding bodies, aren't you?

He signed off after she shared her address, ordered a pizza for pick-up, and shoved his feet into his sneakers. He did his best not to acknowledge how excited he was to hang out with Mallory, but it'd been a long time since he'd socialized without his daughter. Not that talking to moms about gymnastics and princesses wasn't enthralling, but an evening spent talking to someone about other things—and especially someone with Mallory's natural sarcasm and wit—was a welcome change.

Admittedly, the majority of their conversations had been about their parents, Jessica, or pancakes, but he had a feeling once they got to know each other better, he and Mallory would have all kinds of non-family-related things to talk about. That was enticing enough to explain his excitement as he headed over to her place.

When he showed up, pizza and beer in hand, he let out a low whistle at the number of boxes crammed into the small living room.

"I've already gotten the hoarder lecture from my mom," Mal said. "If you're even considering it, just drop the pizza and leave."

"Wouldn't dare." After kicking his shoes off, he followed her through a path deliberately left in the stacks and then sat on the couch next to her.

She handed him a plate. "See? I have managed to unpack a few things." After dropping two slices onto her plate, she folded one in half and took a big bite.

He admired the way she shoved food in her mouth with abandon. He hadn't been on many dates in the last eleven years, but he had been on enough to be tired of watching starved women eat salads or push food around to make it appear as if they'd eaten. His mom was one of those all-natural types, carefully selecting ingredients based on when, where, and how they were grown. She had mostly given up her disappointed sighs and judgment of his dietary choices. He had his dad in his corner now—two against one, and his mother only occasionally won a battle about their affection for junk food. She did still like to remind them with offhand remarks about how they were adults and could eat carcinogens and mistreated animals if they so chose.

Watching Mallory bite into a slice of pizza without questioning where the cheese or sausage came from was pretty damned refreshing.

"What?" she asked around a mouthful.

Phil blinked, clearing his wandering thoughts. "What?"

"You're staring at me." She dragged her palm across her chin. "Do I have sauce on my face? A string of cheese? A hair growing from my chin?"

He chuckled. "No. You're fine. I was just admiring your eating habits."

She stopped chewing and gawked at him.

"I'm being serious. I really like that you aren't afraid to eat."

A smile curved her puffed-out cheeks. "Thanks."

He also folded his slice in half and took a bite before opening two bottles of beer. Looking around at the boxes that surrounded him, he grabbed a napkin to wipe his hands. "Does that say Spider-Man?"

Mallory followed his gaze. "Maybe."

Amused by her seemingly embarrassed response, he narrowed his eyes at her. "Are you a nerd, Mallory?"

"Are you a bully, Phil?"

"Definitely not. But I might be a closet nerd. We were constantly moving around when I was a kid. I never had a lot of things that I could call mine, but I did have a copy of *Captain America: Heroes Reunited,* part four, that I got for my seventh birthday. I read that thing until it fell apart. Man, I loved that comic book."

Her smile returned and light practically started to shine from her eyes. "Best thing about living in San Diego? Comic-Con. Oh my God, it is *insane*. Forget heaven. When I die, I want to go to Comic-Con."

He was tempted to high-five her like he did whenever Jessica said something he got excited about, but he refrained. Then, in that second, he realized his parents were right. He really did need to spend time with someone other than his daughter. Dismissing the thought, he nodded his head toward his find. "So. What's in the Spider-Man box?"

She stared at him, squinting her eyes, clearly weighing her options before dropping the pizza slice and brushing her hands on her jeans. He stood as she peeled the tape back and hesitated one more moment before opening the box. When she did, he thought he heard angels sing. The box was filled with comic books in individually sealed bags.

"Wow," he breathed. Looking at her, he grinned. "You really are a nerd."

She playfully swatted at his shoulder.

"I'm just teasing," he insisted.

"That's not the extent of it."

"No?"

She again faltered, clearly not sure if she wanted to share. "You know I'm a graphic designer, right?"

"You were. Then you moved home and reclaimed your role as a disgruntled real estate agent at your mom's office."

"Hey," she protested. "I never said I was disgruntled."

"Your face did."

She frowned at him. "Let's focus on this. Don't judge me, or I'll never share my secrets with you again." She reached for another box then hefted it up and set it on top of the comics. "This is our secret. If you break my trust, I'll spit on your pizza."

"I wouldn't dream of it."

She opened the second box, and he peered inside at a dozen or so artist's notebooks. She lifted one out then timidly handed the book to him. He flipped the cover open. Page after page of superhero action played out in skillfully hand-drawn images. He was stunned at the depth of her talent.

"You make comic books?" he asked, his voice reflecting his awe.

"I *want* to make comic books," Mallory clarified. "I haven't had much luck yet. You wouldn't think this was such a tough business to break into, but lo and behold, many a nerd would like to have their visions in print. These are just sketches. The finished product is on my computer."

"These are great, Mal." He closed the book and reached for another. After flipping through the pages, he set them in the box and met her gaze. "Is this what you were doing in California? Trying to get a break for your comics?"

She shrugged. "A little. I mean, I've always wanted to do this, but I met people like me—people who like this stuff. Having a tribe fanned the flame. But with Mom..." That strained look returned to her eyes. "I couldn't be there, Phil. Not now. Besides, if I ever get good enough to be published, I don't have to be in California. I can do this from anywhere."

"So you haven't given up?"

She opened one of the books he'd looked at. "No. Of course not. I just... I'm tired of rejection, so I'm taking a break."

He understood. "Rejection is hard."

"Yeah."

"So is having a parent with a sudden onset of disabilities."

She frowned at him, as if she were about to tell him that was a rude comment, but then her face softened. "Yeah, it is. Sometimes it's like... My old mom is trapped inside this broken body, and I feel guilty that I can't help her find a way out." She closed her eyes so tightly that creases formed around them. She shook her head, as if to dislodge the thought. When she met his gaze again, her eyes were filled with a sorrowful look that tugged at his heart. "That sounds horrible, doesn't it?"

"Mallory," he said thoughtfully, "I love my daughter with every cell in my body, but there are times when her life—*my* life —would be easier if she weren't disabled. I can't deny I see that, that I *know* that. But she is disabled, and her disability has given her more strength and compassion than most adults I've ever met. I wouldn't change her for anything. She brings so much happiness to this world, not just to me but to everyone who knows her. Jessica and Annie face challenges we could never fully understand. It's okay to recognize that we wish things were different for them and for us, so long as we accept that things never *will* be different. Jessica will never not have Down, and Annie will never be the way she was before. What matters is that we help them live their lives to the best of their abilities so they can find all the happiness they deserve."

"I know that," she whispered. "Sometimes I just don't know how."

"You don't always have to know, Mal, you just have to try. Your family has had a lot to deal with in a short time."

"You can say that again." She put the book back in the box and flipped the top closed.

"You know, I'm a graphic designer, too. We could use you at Dad's company. We're growing all the time."

She started shaking her head before he finished. "I appreciate that, Phil, but a big reason why I came back to Stonehill was to help Marcus with Mom's agency. He may think he can handle it all alone, but I watched my mom work herself to the bone for years. He can't run the business *and* care for Mom all by himself. It isn't fair for me to expect him to. I did that for too long."

He put his hand to her arm, hating that she was being so hard on herself. "Hey, you are allowed to go out and live your life."

"I know that."

"Do you?" he pressed.

She pulled back under the premise of moving the box she'd opened to another stack. He wasn't sure if she was drawing away from his touch or subtly trying to get him to shut his mouth. Either way, he realized he'd probably pushed the supportive-buddy role too far.

"Yeah. I do," she stated firmly. "I'm not giving up on my art. I'm just putting it on the back burner for a while." Turning to face him, she brushed her hands together before planting them on her hips. "Just until I get settled and can find my footing again."

He hesitated. The last thing he wanted to do was end their friendship before it began because he didn't stop nudging when she clearly wanted him to, but so much was left unsaid. She was clearly struggling more than she wanted anyone to know. Like mother like daughter, if he guessed right.

Instead of pressing the matter any further, he took a page from his father's book of unwavering support for a stubborn woman. "If you need help," he offered, "please let me know. I'm happy to do whatever you need to make this happen."

She smiled, a warm, genuine smile, and some of the shadows left her eyes, letting the light back in. "Thank you. I appreciate that."

CHAPTER FOUR

he following weekend was the deadline Annie had given Mallory. If she hadn't unpacked, her mother was doing it for her. Despite Mallory being an adult with her own home, she had no doubt her mother would show up with her aunt Dianna to sort through all the boxes. She wasn't having that. Instead, she caved and let Phil help her out. She'd already shared her deepest darkest secret, so she didn't see the harm.

As Saturday morning rolled into afternoon, Mallory rested her hands on her hips and slowly turned around. "I don't remember this room being so big."

Phil took in the open space with amazement as if he'd just seen her living area for the first time. Though the house was small, the open concept made the space bright and airy. Between the two of them, they'd filled two bookshelves in her office with comics, set out her photos and an array of tchotchkes, and rearranged her furniture to best suit the room.

"Holy cow," he said with a teasing tone. "Your rental is the TARDIS."

Her heart leaped in her chest as excitement rolled through her. Spinning, widening her eyes as she stared at him, she gasped dramatically. "Did you just make a *Doctor Who* joke?" She pointed at him before he could deny the accusation of making a reference to one of her many sci-fi favorites. "You did. You just implied that my house is bigger on the inside than the outside. You *are* a nerd! I knew it."

He actually blushed a little. "I may have seen a few episodes."

"Favorite Doctor?"

He shrugged, but when she cocked her brows at him, he grinned. "I'm old school. I always liked the Fourth Doctor."

"Tom Baker. Good call. I have to say, I enjoy the newer series a bit more myself. I know a lot of Whovians would disagree, but..." She let her words trail off when his eyes glazed over. Dismissing his boredom with a wave of her hand, she let the topic drop. "Amateur."

Blinking as if his neurons had finally fired, he sighed. "You have to remember who my mother was. Television didn't play a large role in my childhood. We crashed in the guest house of this doctor for one summer while my mom was nannying for them. It was by the ocean. I would have stayed there forever. I learned to surf that summer. And I watched a lot of TV, even a little *Doctor Who*."

"Well. Lucky for you, I happen to own the *entire* collection to get you caught up. Start to present."

He opened his mouth as if he were going to disagree but then seemed to think better of it. He peered out the big window. "Is that Annie and Marcus?"

Mallory's heart dropped to her stomach. The last thing she needed was her mom catching Phil in her living room. Not that her friendship with Phil was a secret, but the *other* last thing Mallory needed was her mother getting the wrong idea about them. Not that there was a wrong idea. But... A quick glance confirmed the car pulling to the curb in front of her house was Marcus's. "Shit."

Facing Phil, Mallory debated having him sneak out the back door like she had done once to her high school boyfriend. Her mom had come home from work for lunch during summer break, and Mallory had just worked up the courage to let her boyfriend take off her shirt. She would have gotten away with sneaking him in while her mom was at work if only he'd grabbed his shoes on the way out. Mallory tried to be casual, but Annie sniffed out the evidence like a cadaver dog. She scooped up the boy's shoes, eyed her daughter, and Mallory broke down in a fit of tears and hiccups.

After that dreadful episode, she'd been forced to spend every summer day and after-school hour at O'Connell Realty. She'd learned all about folding brochures and filing listings. Her mother had paid her, so her time wasn't exactly wasted, but she'd still felt imprisoned. She'd never been trusted to be home alone again after a pair of men's shoes had spontaneously appeared in their house.

"Men are only after one thing, Mallory Jane," Annie had stated that day. "And you're too young to give it."

Mal was an adult now. There was no need to rush a shoe-less Phil out the back door and hope her mother didn't catch on. She had every right to have a man in her house. *Her* house. Even so, her stomach knotted with the same fear she'd felt as Donny Snider had run away in his bare feet. Looking at Phil, she lifted her hands as if to soothe him. "Just be cool."

He lifted his brows in question. "Why wouldn't I be cool?"

"I mean... Remember how you said your mom had added me to your pool of potential significant others?" She lifted her shoulders high in an apologetic shrug. "You're about to get tossed into my pool. Probably head first. And weighed down so you can't escape. My mom really likes you. Well...your kid. You're just part of the Jessica package."

He shrugged, much as she had. "Hey, you could do worse." Smiling, he called down the hall to the office where they had set Jess up with colored pencils and a sketchbook. "Annie's here, Punk."

Fast as the Flash, the girl ran through the living room and out the front door. Mallory and Phil watched her reach the car just as Marcus was helping Annie out. Jessica took Annie's hand, talking a mile a minute, and guided her into the house, leaving Marcus behind. Mallory had some strange realization, something about how while having Annie as a mother was a bit like having the Terminator standing over her shoulder most of her life, the woman had so much love and protectiveness inside her. She would be a wonderful grandmother. Especially to Jessica, since they had such a strong bond already.

The thought spread through Mallory's chest like the first big gulp of bourbon, warming her from the inside out before settling in her stomach with a punch.

She physically shuddered, forcing the thought away. She'd never really considered that she might want a family someday, but the image before her seemed to have kicked a part of her she had never acknowledged existed. Pushing the odd thought far, far from her mind, she faced Phil. "I give Mom five minutes before she's trying to get me alone so she can ask why you're here."

He scoffed. "No way she's going to make it that long. I give her less than two minutes."

She opened the timer on her watch, ready to press the button to make it start as soon as Annie walked in the door. "Loser buys pizza. And...go."

Jessica pushed the front door open, saying, "Do you know that Mallory has comic books?"

"Wait. What?" Mallory whispered. "Why is she ratting me out?"

"Like a *gazillion* of them," Jessica continued.

"Oh, she can't keep secrets," Phil said under his breath.

"Now you tell me."

Annie walked in, but Mallory doubted the questions in her eyes were about the aforementioned comic book collection. Her mother was staring at Phil, obviously wondering why he was there. Crap. No way she was going to make it five minutes before asking what she was clearly trying to sort out. With any luck, Jessica would distract her longer than two minutes.

However, with pizza riding on this bet, Mallory decided not to leave it up to luck.

"I'm so glad you're here," she said to her parents, who cast curious glances at each other. Okay, that might have been laying it on a little thick. She never made a big deal about them popping in. Gesturing around, she tried to turn their focus on the living room. "Check this out, huh?"

"Nice," Annie said and then nailed her daughter down with that mind-piercing stare of hers. "Why don't we let Marcus catch up with Phil while you show me the rest."

Damn it.

Phil grabbed Mallory's wrist and chuckled as he checked the timer. "Less than a minute."

Jerking her arm away from his grasp, she scowled. "Nobody likes a braggart."

Annie lifted her brows and smiled, and Mallory knew the battle was lost. Might as well come clean now.

"Phil and Jessica offered to help me unpack without judgmental commentary on how many possessions I own. *Mom.*"

Holding her hands up, as if to show her innocence, Annie said, "I never said a word."

"You might have said one or two," Marcus countered.

Annie elbowed him while Mallory thanked him for his support.

"Come see," Jessica insisted, tugging at Annie's hand.

Mallory wanted to protest, but the proverbial cat had been released from the bag. Annie continued to eye Mallory, obviously more interested in her company than in the books Jessica wanted to show.

"Remember that you can't take the comics from the bags," Phil warned.

Jessica rolled her eyes. "I *know*, Daddy. Mallory told me the rules."

Marcus opened his mouth. He was more discreet than her mother, but he wasn't afraid to pry into her life. Now that Annie was out of the way, she had no doubt that he was going to start pushing his own brand of nosiness on her.

"Phil needs help hanging curtains," Mallory stated before her stepdad could say a word. "I'm too short."

Give Marcus a chore, and he would be thoroughly distracted until it was done. He turned, looking at the rods still sitting next to the window. "I can do that." However, even with a distraction dangling like a carrot, he nodded his head toward the hallway where Jessica had dragged Annie. "You go answer your mother's questions so I don't have to hear her hashing this out all night."

"Fine." Leaving the men to their task, Mal headed to her office. She was already thinking of ways to distract Annie, but that process came to an immediate halt. When she was a kid, fascinated by comic books, her mom had dismissed those conversations with a pat on the head and a few muted comments as she focused on her work. She was always focused on her work.

As a single mother building a business and raising a child, she never seemed to have a lot of time for Mallory's hobbies. Annie had sacrificed a lot to make a secure home and future for Mallory. She'd been angry and resentful of her mom's business when she was younger. She'd spent a lot of time as a kid feeling like she was second to a bunch of houses, but she grew up to understand her mother had been fighting an uphill battle for years to keep a roof over their heads.

As she rounded the corner, Mallory was completely taken aback. All those years that she'd thought her mother hadn't heard her disappeared as Annie explained to Jessica why it was so important to not touch the pages. The comics were collector's editions; fingerprints and creases made them less valuable. The bags protected them and kept them safe. But the zinger was when she explained that Mallory had been collecting the comics since she was a teenager and they were really important to her.

Mallory hadn't realized Annie had known. She'd kept her ongoing love of the books a secret because she felt like she should have outgrown the childish fascination. Leaning against the doorjamb, she crossed her arms and listened until Jessica noticed her.

"This is so cool, Mal," she said. "I'm going to have a comic book collection someday, too. And a room to keep them all in."

"Well, you'd better get started," Mallory said. "It takes a long time to get this many." She pushed off the doorframe and walked into the office. "I'm going to a really cool event next weekend with comic books. Maybe you could ask your dad if you can go with me."

Jessica widened her eyes and drew a gasping breath. She was gone in a blink, screaming for Phil as she ran down the hall.

Turning her focus to her mother, Mallory chuckled. "I don't think she's going to leave him much choice."

"Not likely." Putting the book back on the shelf, Annie lifted her brows and waited.

Mallory moaned. "Don't start, Mom."

"I didn't."

"You did. Internally," Mallory clarified.

Annie smiled. "Phil's nice."

Heaving a dramatic sigh, much like those that Jessica loved to give her father, Mallory pointed out, "All my friends are nice. Even the ones who are boys."

"You've got nice friends. But Phil is the only one here, isn't he?"

This wasn't the end of Annie's inquisition. Mallory wasn't foolish enough to believe that, but she did hope that she'd be tactful enough to let it drop for now. "I've got some clothes to hang. Want to help?"

sh

Phil tossed the crust of his third slice of pizza onto his plate. "This was probably the best-tasting pizza I've ever had."

"Don't rub it in," Mallory warned.

Jessica didn't respond. Mallory had spread a blanket on the floor in front of the television and given her the big slice of pizza in the box, despite Phil's protest that she'd never eat that much. Her eyes had been glued to the television ever since Phil had agreed she could watch an old live-action He-Man film from Mallory's movie collection...the size of which very nearly rivaled her comic books.

"You've created a monster." He nodded toward his daughter. "She's going to pester you to death about all this comic book stuff."

"There are worse things to be pestered about. I'm glad she likes them."

He had to admit this was a heck of a better preoccupation than some of the other things Jessica got fixated on. Maybe he'd be lucky and this would be the thing to finally break the My Little Pony streak that had been going for far too long as far as he was concerned. He remembered seeing the little pastel-colored horses during his childhood, but he hadn't expected them to come back around for his own child to obsess about.

"So about this comic book convention—" he started.

"I can take her if you don't want to go," Mallory offered. "I mean, if that's okay with you. I promise to keep an eye on her. She won't leave my side."

"I'll go."

She widened her eyes, obviously stunned by his statement. "Really?"

"Yeah. Really. It might be fun."

Her smile grew and that light filled her eyes again. He really liked when she got excited. She practically glowed. In a way, her excitement reminded him of Jessica's. When Jessica was happy, she couldn't hide it. Mallory was that way. He liked that about her.

"Do you have a costume?" she asked.

"A…a costume?"

"Yeah." She put her plate down, dragged her hands over her jeans, and snatched up her phone.

While she tapped the screen, Phil fought the urge to tell her to use napkins. He'd been trying to pound that into Jessica's head for so long, the words almost slipped before he caught them. He managed to swallow them down. Mallory was a grown-up, and if she wanted to ruin her clothes with greasy pizza stains, that was her right.

Turning her smartphone to him, she said, "See? Everyone dresses up."

"I want to be a My Little Pony," Jessica announced. Clearly her focus hadn't been as singular as Phil had thought.

"You'll be the best pony ever," Mallory announced.

Jessica broke her hypnotic gaze from the television long enough to smile at Mallory but then went back to eating and watching He-Man save the universe.

"The pink one is your favorite, huh, Punk?"

She nodded but didn't turn away from the images playing out on screen.

Mallory scrolled on her phone again before showing him a picture of a girl around Jessica's age dressed in a costume that seemed easy enough. He nodded his approval or agreement or whatever Mallory was looking for.

"Does she have pink tights and a leotard?"

"Yup."

"Sweet. I can get her a wig before next week. Done. Easy-peasy. Now." She focused on him. "What do you want to be? A purple pony?"

Jessica giggled but didn't respond. Phil, however, cast Mallory a playful glare.

"No ponies for me. I'll find something."

She lifted her gaze from her phone, and disbelief danced around her face. From the sagging jaw to the lifted brows to the confusion in her eyes, everything said she didn't trust him with this task. "Don't be lame, Phil."

"Scout's honor."

"Were you a Scout?"

He considered his past for a moment. "Hippie's honor."

Her soft laugh was damn near musical. He was glad to see some of the stress had left her. When she'd first returned to Stonehill, he'd been worried about her, about the strain he'd seen in her eyes. Being home was good for her. Maybe she was right when she'd said that she just needed to be closer to family. Phil couldn't imagine not living close to his parents now that he had them both.

Some people were just more family-oriented than others. He admired that Mallory understood her need to be close to the people she had been connected to her entire life. He knew from Dianna, his mother's best friend, that the O'Connell clan was pretty tight. Phil had first met Mallory at the lakefront home where her uncle Paul and Dianna were married. The wedding had been simple but filled with family and laughter.

Kara and Harry's wedding had a similar setting, but theirs had been filled with tension and bickering between their two families as to who was more to blame for Kara spending thirty years away from Stonehill—her parents for disowning her or his parents for sending her to a home for unwed mothers. In the end, Kara lashed out, she and Harry fought, and the two ended up leaving the wedding without telling anyone so they could start their marriage with some sort of sense of peace.

The O'Connell gathering, on the other hand, was the first time Phil had seen so many blood relatives happy to be around each other. It was refreshing and...odd.

"What was it like growing up with so much family around?" he asked, unable to keep his curiosity to himself.

Mallory laughed flatly, but the love in her eyes was obvious. "I never got away with anything. I didn't have a dad around, but Mom was on top of things. And if she missed something, I had uncles more than happy to step in and keep me in check. I don't remember much about my grandpa, but I know my mom and uncles didn't care for him much. We didn't see him very often. He passed when I was little, but my uncles were always there. Looming, watching..."

"Protecting," Phil offered.

She considered his suggestion for a moment before nodding. "Yes. Protecting. What about you? You must have seen some amazing things being a drifter child."

He snickered. "Drifter child? I guess that's one way to put it." He turned on the plush gray sofa, the one that was far too nice for Jessica to eat pizza on, so he could more easily see Mallory. "I hated it. I resented it. Of course, now that I'm older, I know there were some benefits. I *did* see amazing things. I met some amazing people with incredible stories to tell. The problem was, by the time I formed a bond with any of them, Mom was packing us up to move again."

"She couldn't sit still long, huh?"

"Still can't, really. She's always talking about the places she wants to visit when she and Harry have time. They fly to Oregon once a year to visit the commune where she still has a lot of friends. That was the place his mother sent her when she was pregnant with me."

Mallory creased her brow but was kind enough not to bash his grandparents. The choices they'd made were decades old now, and the Martinson-Canton clan had rehashed them more than enough times on their own.

"Mom never took me anywhere," Mallory said. "She was so

focused on building up the security she'd never had that we didn't get to have much fun."

Phil felt a pang. Wasn't that exactly what his mom said he was guilty of doing to Jessica? He dismissed the idea as quickly as it occurred to him. "It paid off. Her real estate company is doing really well."

"Yeah. Her stint in the hospital could have cost her everything if she hadn't spent so many years preparing for the worst-case scenario. She was lucky in that regard."

He took a breath before making a confession. "I'm probably going to sound like an ass saying this, but I'd never really given much thought to how much my mom means to me until you talked to me about how scary it was to almost lose Annie. My mom has always been so hard to handle, I grew up feeling like I was barely surviving her insanity. I've been trying to be better about appreciating that she's just different."

Mallory smiled brightly as she patted his knee. "She's fun. She really is, Phil. She's so kind and unique."

"Yeah. Unique gets old for a kid who wants normal."

"But you're not a kid anymore," she said gently.

"No. I'm not. And I've been thinking about what I'd lose if something ever happened to her. And I did that because of you, so thanks for that."

"I'm glad you could benefit from my personal hell."

He grabbed her hand before she could pull away and squeezed her fingers. The amusement in her eyes faded into concern or maybe confusion. "I just meant that I probably would have kept resenting her antics until it was too late for me to realize I needed to look at her through a different light. She works hard to keep our family going. She always has, even when our family was just the two of us. Now she looks out for Harry and both of my grandmothers, as well as Jess and me."

"And that cranky baby," Mallory reminded him.

"And that unnaturally cranky baby."

Mallory turned her focus to Jessica, and Phil knew her next question before she asked.

"Her mother left because she was scared." Sliding closer so they could lower their voices, decreasing the chance of Jessica eavesdropping, he whispered, "She was scared about becoming a mother before we knew about her disabilities. Jessica having Down syndrome just tipped the scale. The stress got to be too much. Jess had to have open-heart surgery when she was an infant, and that was it. The last emotional hit Katrina could take. She walked out and never looked back."

"Do you ever hear from her?"

"No. It's better that way." Looking at Jessica, verifying that she was still watching the TV, he said, "She's too sensitive to rejection to have someone walking in and out of her life. She's better off without that woman."

Sympathy filled Mallory's face—her eyes softened, and her smile was sweet. "I'm sorry, Phil. That couldn't have been easy for you."

"I was too worried about my daughter to care what she did. Everything worked out for the best. I believe that. Jessica is stronger for it in some ways, but I know she still feels the loss."

"She did mention it to me once. I told her I didn't have a dad until Mom and Marcus got married." She giggled then, and her smile changed from supportive to mischievous. "She doesn't think you'll ever get married though because you're too particular."

He rolled his eyes but didn't disagree. "Dating is for losers."

"Agreed."

Happy they saw eye to eye on that topic as well, he settled back on the couch to finish watching the movie and let the sense of contentment settle over him.

CHAPTER FIVE

*P*hil crossed his arms and stood blocking the doorway to the bathroom across the hallway from Jessica's bright pink bedroom. This room would be pink too, if she'd had her way, but he'd informed her that the only room she got to paint was her own. The bathroom was for her and their guests, and not everyone appreciated the color as much as she did.

The girl hadn't stopped rambling as Mallory applied her face paint. Phil was amazed Mallory was able to paint the girl's cheeks at all, but every few minutes, she'd take a deep breath and Jess would do the same. As they held their breath, Mallory would make quick swipes along Jessica's cheeks and chin. She'd then focus on Jessica's forehead as they talked and talked and talked. He couldn't help but laugh at the pair. They seemed to be as close as best friends could be already. His chuckle drew a frown from his daughter.

"Daddy's being a party pooper," Jessica announced.

Mallory nodded her head. "He certainly is."

Phil looked down at his Superman T-shirt, black jeans, and Converse. "This is as close to *cosplay* as I get."

"Party pooper," Jess and Mal said at the same time. The pair giggled, and Phil shook his head in faux dismay.

Mallory adjusted Jessica's costume one more time then stood. "All right, m'lady. Are you ready to see how amazing you look?"

"Ready!"

Mallory turned the girl toward the mirror, and Jessica gasped loudly. "I look just like a My Little Pony!"

Mal straightened the pink wig a bit. "Yes, ma'am, you do."

"Thank you!" She gave Mallory a big hug.

Phil couldn't help but laugh when Mallory put her fingertip to Jessica's forehead, stopping her before the girl left a pink face-print on Mal's stomach.

"Hey! Careful of that masterpiece. You don't want to smudge."

When Mallory had first started dressing Jessica up, he almost protested, wondering just how long it would take to get the glitter makeup off his kid's cheeks. But at the excitement on Jessica's face as she went on and on about how much fun they were going to have at the comic book convention and how Annie had given her ten whole dollars to buy her first comic book, Phil kept his objections to himself.

He couldn't remember the last time his daughter had been this wound up about something. Sure, she was always bubbly and happy, but this was a kind of raw enthusiasm he hadn't seen in a long time. She looked like she really could burst from the anticipation of getting to the comic book convention.

Phil was amazed by how much Mallory had influenced Jessica already. His daughter was borderline giddy, and her happiness was certainly contagious. Mallory hadn't stopped smiling along with her, explaining what kinds of things they might see and nicely reminding Jessica how important it was to stay close to her or Phil the entire time. She did it without nagging or making Jessica get defensive, the way she did when he told her.

"There will be so many people there," Mallory warned her. "You have to be really careful to stay close, okay?"

"Okay." That was her only response. No eye roll, no dramatic sigh, no lecture about how she wasn't a baby anymore. Just *okay*.

Jessica and Mallory had obviously become quick friends, and the respect between them was mutual. Mallory's interest in Jessica seemed genuine. Phil hadn't asked, but he suspected Mallory felt bonded to Jessica because the girl had developed such a bond with Annie. Jessica was protective of Annie, which amused Phil, considering Annie was the adult. Jessica said she understood how Annie felt—how it made her sad when people couldn't decipher her words or tried to help her because they assumed she couldn't do things for herself. Jessica had been dealing with that all her life and was the first to jump to Annie's defense when someone tried to coddle her.

That was something Mallory confessed to struggling with.

Jessica seemed to be teaching her how to handle Annie's disabilities as much as Mallory was teaching her how to be carefree and silly. Something Phil definitely had forgotten how to be years ago.

Jessica darted out of the bathroom. "Come on, guys. We don't want to be late. I bet nobody else is going to be dressed like me."

Phil helped Mallory, who was dressed as a female version of Wolverine, close a few of the face paints. When the paints were securely back in her unicorn-shaped bag, zippered by the rainbow-colored tail, she put her hands on her hips, and he skimmed his gaze over her. She looked hilariously adorable.

She looked him over as well, but she didn't look amused. She frowned and shook her head. "I can't believe that's what you're wearing."

"Says the girl wearing the bright yellow unitard and muttonchops."

She kept her face deadpan as she slid plastic fangs into her mouth. "Last chance, Dad. You putting on that Batman costume I brought you or what?"

"Not a chance."

"Loser," she said, lisping the word out around the fake teeth.

Brushing by him, she headed into his living room, where Jessica was shoving her feet into her boots, still rambling about how much fun the convention was going to be. Phil stood back and watched Mallory help her into her coat. She kneeled down to zip it for her so the long pink wig didn't get caught. His stomach did a funny little flip thing when Jessica hugged Mallory again, being more careful of her makeup this time, just as Mal had warned her.

The image was almost perfect, almost exactly what Phil had thought their life would have been had Katrina not run out, had Phil not been so focused on Jessica that he skipped over ever bringing another woman into their lives...had a million things happened differently. He could have sworn he heard his mother's voice in his head, whispering about how Jessica needed someone in her life to teach her all the things Katrina should have.

No way in hell would he have ever dressed Jessica like a pink pony and taken her to a comic book convention. That wasn't really his idea of fun, but the smile on Jessica's face said it all—she was eating this up and would be reliving this day for years to come. Frowning, he looked down at his jeans and T-shirt. Maybe he really was a stick in the mud. He was the only one not bubbling over with excitement. Maybe he did just need to relax and go with the flow more.

Damn it. He hated when his mother was right.

Mallory put her hands on her yellow-spandex-covered hips again. "You coming?"

He rolled his eyes, more out of disbelief at the words that were about to come from his mouth than anything else. "Yeah. Just...just let me change first."

"Yes," Mallory hissed and then turned and gave Jessica a high five.

Within a few minutes, he was dressed like a superhero. With the intent of going out in public. What the hell was he thinking?

As he drove them to the convention center, Phil felt more like a parental escort than a member of the party. Jessica had spent the week learning about comic books. She and Mallory were having a conversation he wasn't fully up-to-date on. He knew enough to know what they were talking about but not enough to contribute any insight. He was going to have to work on that, he suspected. This topic likely wasn't going away anytime soon.

When he parked the car, he was prepared to give Jessica the "don't run off" lecture he gave any time they went to a festival or show where there were crowds of people, but she snagged Mallory's hand and stuck to her side like glue. The two pointed and gasped and *oohed* and *ahhed* every time they saw someone else in costume.

After paying for tickets and looking around the big room filled with every kind of fictional, anime, and cartoon character imaginable, Mallory gave Phil the same told-you-so smirk his mother so often used on him.

"Don't say it," he mumbled.

Mal laughed and slid her arm through his, tugging him playfully. "Come on, Batdad, admit how happy you are that you didn't wear plain ol' jeans and a T-shirt."

"I'm very glad."

She nodded toward the big graffiti-style sign announcing the convention. "I need pictures. Go on, you two, get over there."

"You, too, Mal," Jessica pleaded, not letting go of her hand.

She started to argue, but Phil pulled out his phone. "Go on. I don't need pictures."

"Oh, hardly," Mallory disagreed. "Excuse me, Captain Kirk." She smiled when a man turned and faced her. "Would you take a picture of us, please?"

Phil wanted to warn her about handing her phone to strangers, but she didn't hesitate. She was too trusting. He didn't have time to lecture her about securing her personal belongings, because she had his hand and was dragging him to the sign. With Jessica between them, posing like a professional My Little Pony model, they smiled and the man took a few pictures.

Though he handed the phone right back to Mallory, Phil said under his breath, "He could have taken off with your phone, you know that, right?"

"Yes, I know. I prefer to trust people, Phil. The world looks brighter that way. Besides, most of these people are so deep in character, all I'd have to do is yell and someone would have tackled him to save the day." She bumped him gently. "Let your overwhelming sense of responsibility go and try to have fun for just a few hours. Please."

Her words stung. The rug seemed to have been pulled out from under him for a moment. Was that how she saw him? Overly responsible? Too serious? Too...boring to have fun? He knew that was how his mom saw him, but his mom was the reason he was like this. Someone had to be the grown-up. Jessica saw him that way, too, but he was her father. He was supposed to set rules and boundaries.

However, he hadn't realized Mallory saw him like that. That struck him in a way he hadn't expected. He didn't want her to see him as the party pooper she'd accused him of being earlier. She liked to have fun, and he wanted her to see him as someone she could have fun with. He followed a few paces behind as Mallory and Jessica took in the convention with blatant awe and excitement. Following Jessica's pointed finger, he watched a unicorn walk by and tried to see the magic in the moment the way they obviously were.

He tried to see beyond an adult dressed like a white horse with a horn stuck on its head to the majesty of the moment. Disappointment flooded his mind as, instead, he focused on how there was dirt on the knee and the rainbow mane was a tangled mess. He guessed he never really had seen the world through the lens that Jessica and Mallory, or even his mom, did. His mind was analytical like his father's, but even Harry had the ability to appreciate the beauty of the world. He'd stand back and stare at Kara's artwork with amazement, seeing the splendor in what she'd created. Phil had always thought that was just because he was so in love with Kara, but maybe there was something to her art that he'd just never seen before. He'd have to look again.

"Hey," Mallory said, bringing him back from his reflection. "Come on. You can't be that bored. We've been here for like ten minutes."

Instead of confessing that he was perplexed by his lack of

enjoyment, he nodded toward a table where a mermaid was selling food. "I was wondering what kind of goodies we might find over there."

Mallory followed his gaze. "Food. I like food."

He led them to the table and let Jessica pick out three cookies, making her promise not to eat them until after lunch, which he suspected would be soon—and expensive, based on the cost of the baked goods. He swallowed down the complaint, though. This was their fun time. Their family time. A much-needed good time. He wasn't going to allow a price tag to take away from that. Not today.

As he handed over far more cash than the cookies were worth, he promised himself that he'd take his overwhelming-responsibility hat off and have fun. Real fun. Even if it killed him.

sh

"The most important thing to remember when you wear makeup," Mallory said while wiping a cloth over Jessica's face, "is to take it off. Never, ever sleep in makeup."

"Because you ruin your pillows."

"And your skin," Mallory added. She went through three washrags but finally got all the face paint and most of the glitter from Jessica's skin. Smiling at the rosy-pink cheeks, she had to stop herself from giving the girl a big kiss on the head. That was probably crossing the line, but man, she just wanted to scoop her up and hug her. "Did you have a good day?" she whispered instead.

"I had the best day," Jess said just as softly, as if they were conspiring.

"I'm going to put the best pictures together and make a poster for you, okay?"

Her eyes went wide. "Awesome."

While Mallory had hesitated in squeezing Jessica, the girl didn't. She lurched forward and wrapped her arms around Mal's neck, hugging her like she'd never let go. Mallory hugged back, and maybe they wouldn't have ever let go, but Phil called from across the hall.

"Come on, Jess. It's getting late."

Leaning back, Mallory tapped Jess on the tip of the nose. "Thank you for being my best convention partner ever."

"Thank you for being *my* best convention partner ever."

"I can't wait to go again."

"Me either. Night, Mal."

"Night, Jess." Once the girl left the room, Mallory closed the door and wriggled out of her costume back into regular clothes. The hard part, however, was peeling the fake muttonchops off her cheeks. She ground her teeth and hissed as the glue ripped out strands of her hair and stuck to her skin. Finally, she was free of the fake hair and most of the adhesive, though her cheeks were even pinker than Jessica's had been after scrubbing away all her glitter.

She eased the door open and tiptoed down the hallway so she

didn't disturb Jessica and Phil's routine. She could hear his voice traveling down the hall as he talked to his little girl. She thought maybe he was reading her a story, but Jessica seemed too big for that. Whatever they were doing, Mallory had the urge to peek in and see if she could take part. She resisted, however, and focused on gathering her things so she could head out once she said goodbye to Phil.

"She's out," he said, coming into his living room several minutes later. Phil, dressed in his jeans and Superman T-shirt again, strolled in looking far more relaxed than she could remember seeing him. Ever. "She's pretty proud of her new comic books. Looks like I'll be getting a second job to keep her in supply."

"Whoops." She wasn't sorry, though. She was thrilled she and Jessica would continue to have something to bond over. "I'm surprised she made it as long as she did. It's been a long day. I'm surprised at you, too."

"Me?"

"We spent almost six hours at that convention, and you looked like you were enjoying yourself."

He started to object—she could tell by the raised brows—but then he laughed. "I had a really good time, Mal. So did Jessica. Thanks for inviting us."

"Thank you for dressing up as Batman. I think that made her day even better."

"I don't want to see any of those photos on social media."

She smiled wide and batted her eyes innocently. "It *may* be too late for that."

"Great."

He laughed softly then reached out and ran his finger over her cheek. Adhesive from where she'd attached the fake hair to her face balled and rolled along her skin until he pulled it off. It was a very paternal move, something he'd probably do to Jessica, except that when he met Mallory's eyes again, his smile faded, confirming in her mind that he'd also felt that strange little electrical jolt that rushed through her skin when he'd touched her.

She hoped there was more glue or glitter. Hell, she'd even take a bit of dried nacho cheese from one of the many trips to the snack bar she'd made. Anything to get him to run his fingers along her flesh again. He didn't but instead balled up the glue as an eternity seemed to pass before she could think again. Clearing her throat, she returned her focus to her bag, overflowing from the loot she'd snatched up at the convention.

"Um... Your mom was very impressed that we got you to dress up. I told her you did it for Jess."

"Oh, man," he moaned. "She saw the pictures?"

"On Facebook."

"You're Facebook friends with my mom?"

She held up her hand, fingers crossed. "We've been like *this* ever since she saw us at breakfast two weeks ago."

He exhaled loudly. "You're kidding me."

"Nope. After seeing Jessica's getup today, she asked if I can help her with the next school play. Apparently she does the costumes to help out."

"She does, but her reasoning isn't quite that generous. She wants an excuse to keep an eye on Jessica and make sure she's being included. Mom still doesn't think Jess can fend for herself. I'm sorry she roped you in."

"Don't be. It'll be fun. Your mom is sweet."

"And nosy."

"And nosy. But I can tell she's just worried about Jessica."

"Yes. That's the only reason I haven't completely lost my cool with her yet. However, you realize she'll never let me live this down, right?"

Her heart lifted as she imagined all the Batman jokes she was going to get out of this day, too. "Yeah. I know. That's okay. I put pictures of Wolverine out there, too. Jessica was there, so use her as an excuse. You did it for the kiddo."

He narrowed his eyes playfully. "Are you confessing to using my daughter as a means to justify dressing up as a comic book hero?"

"Oh, no. I was going to go with or without you guys. I never need an excuse to dress up as a comic book hero. Take that as a warning. If you ever show up unannounced, who knows what I'll be wearing."

His eyes lit with a bit of mischievousness. "Sounds dangerous."

For a moment she thought he might be flirting. Phil flirting? With her? The idea made her heart race, but she also felt a huge rush of uncertainty. She'd never been good at reading or responding to flirtatious behavior. Instead of making a fool of herself and responding incorrectly, she reached into her bag and pulled out a surprise for him. "I found this today. My way of saying thank you for wearing pointy ears and a mask."

Phil hesitated before taking the brown paper bag from her. Peering inside, his smile widened as he pulled out the comic book. "Are you kidding me?"

"Don't—" Before she could get the words out, he had the plastic torn from around the comic book and had started flipping through the pages of *Captain America: Heroes Reunited,* part four. Maybe she should have reminded him of the rules of comic book collecting. Jessica had them down pat, but Phil seemed unaware of the distress his fingers on the pages was causing. So much for it being a collector's edition someday.

She shrugged. Not everyone wanted to stash the books on a shelf. Some people wanted to enjoy the masterpieces they owned. "You said it was your favorite when you were a kid, so when I saw it, I thought you should have it."

"You remembered that?"

"Sure. Why wouldn't I?"

"I don't know."

He flipped through the pages again, wearing a smile bigger than she'd ever seen on him. He always seemed so serious, but she was confident he had a spunky side just waiting to come out. Somehow he had convinced himself he wasn't supposed to have fun, but she'd seen his serious exterior crack over the course of the convention. She'd made progress today. If she kept pushing the fun button, maybe someday it would take and he'd realize he could be a grown-up *and* have a good time. At least as far as Mallory was concerned.

"Thanks," he said genuinely, his smile still bright. "Thank you. This is very cool. And thanks for taking us with you today. Jessica really did have a good time."

"Yes, she did. So did I." She bit her lip, suddenly at a loss for things to say.

He was still grinning like a kid at...well, a kid at a comic book convention. Her chest felt a little tingly at the knowledge that she was the one who had made him so happy.

The tingles were replaced by another awkward silence when he looked up and their gazes locked. She was saved when her phone rang. Reaching into her back pocket, she pulled it out and looked at the screen, even though she knew by the ringtone it was her mother. "Hey, Mom."

"Hey. What are you doing?" Annie asked, speaking slowly and enunciating her words as she tended to do on the phone. She'd learned that the little speaker blended her words if she talked too fast.

"Just getting ready to head home from Phil's. We took Jessica to the comic book convention."

"I saw the pictures. You looked so cute."

"Cute? Mom, I was dressed like Wolverine. He's brutal."

"Well, you didn't look brutal. You looked adorable."

Mallory rolled her eyes and grinned at Phil. "I did not look adorable."

He whispered, "Yes, you did."

She narrowed her eyes at him. "I looked ferocious."

He shook his head, and she gently shoved his shoulder.

"So you're still at Phil's?" Annie asked.

"For a few more minutes."

"Well. I should let you go. Will you come over tomorrow? I want to hear all about today."

Mallory's smile changed from amused to a smirk. She should have seen this coming a mile away. "There's not a lot to tell, Mom. We dressed up like goofballs and hung out with other goofballs."

"I bet Jessica thought it was great," Annie said.

"She did think it was great."

"And it looked like you were having fun."

Mallory sighed as she actually felt her mother luring her into a trap. "We did have fun."

"Good. So come over and tell me all about it."

"I'll see you tomorrow, Mom." She ended the call and slid the phone back into her jeans pocket. "Do you feel like you're drowning yet?"

Phil chuckled. "Yes, I imagine my mom will be cornering me as well. Maybe you'll think twice before posting our outings on social media."

She grabbed her bag and tossed it over her shoulder. "Unlike you, I have the nerve to tell my mom we're just friends."

"Hey, I've told my mom that. She doesn't listen. And let me remind you, your mom is about ten times more stubborn than my mom, so good luck convincing her otherwise."

"Only ten times?" she deadpanned before heading for the door. "I think you underestimate my mother."

CHAPTER SIX

From the moment Jessica woke up, she'd begged Phil to take her to show her grandparents her new comic books. She'd gotten three of them. One from the money Annie gave her, one as a gift from Mallory, and one that Phil agreed to buy. Not to mention all the other expensive knickknacks she'd convinced him to purchase. Now he sat at his mother's table with her smirking like a know-it-all.

Phil didn't think it was possible, but Jessica finally got tired of talking about Mallory and ran off to show Grandpa her comic books once again. Kara didn't say a word as she pretended to focus on Mira, but that damned smile of hers said more than enough.

"Stop it," Phil warned his mother.

She batted bright blue doe eyes at him. "What?"

"Thinking what you're thinking."

She opened her mouth wide, faking shock, but a smirk twitched at her lips. "What was I thinking?"

"Whatever it is that you've been thinking since the first time you saw me and Jessica sitting with Mallory at the café." He shook his head, mainly out of frustration that he'd been thinking it too much lately, too. Not thinking about *them* seriously, but the idea that Mallory was pretty and really was good for Jessica had danced around his mind for a minute or two after their day at the convention.

After she'd left the night before and the house was quiet, he had that strange sense of loneliness he was determined to deny had been happening more and more often. He'd crawled into his bed, and it seemed far too large. Much too empty. He'd been tempted to call Mallory and invite her back over. But for what reason? To have a late-night snack and movie so he didn't have to be alone? Oh, that would have been rich. She never would have let him live that down.

He couldn't help but wonder if he would have wanted to live it down. The idea of her crashing on one side of the bed, probably eating chips or some other crumbly thing that would have left a mess in her wake, would have been worth whatever teasing mockery she tossed at him. He didn't think having her munching on a snack and talking faster than he could register as they stretched out in bed was such a bad idea. Actually, that seemed like a great idea. A perfect idea. The perfect end to what had been the perfect day.

"Looks like you guys had a good time," Kara said, pulling his attention back to her.

"We did."

She continued to focus on Mira. "You dressed up as Batman."

"For Jessica," he clarified.

Kara finally looked at him. "Oh, I know. You wouldn't do anything just for the fun of it, would you?"

He toasted her with his cup of fresh-squeezed orange juice. "Thanks for reminding me I'm lame."

"Well, your main goal as a teenager was to rain on my parade."

"I wasn't raining on your parade, Mom. One of us had to act like an adult."

She wrinkled her nose at him, but there was a happy twinkle in her eyes. "Oh, look at that. The old resentments still burn."

Some of his defensiveness faded—most of it, if Phil were being honest. "You brought it up. And, no, they don't. I know I've always given you crap, but I'm over it. That's all done. I just don't want to hear this."

She pulled the near-empty bottle from Mira's little mouth. Phil braced himself, but the babe puckered a few times before drifting off to sleep. He didn't think she'd ever looked that peaceful before.

"You don't want to hear what?" she asked.

"How you think Mallory O'Connell is so good for me."

Kara lifted her gaze as she gently rested Mira against her shoulder. Phil thought he actually saw her maternal gears working. "You seem to be spending quite a bit of time with her lately. Am I not supposed to notice that?"

"Yes, we are spending a lot of time with her. Jessica likes her. But that doesn't mean what you're thinking."

Patting the baby's back, she grinned. "And what am I thinking?"

"That I should keep Mallory. Like a pet."

"Well, she is beautiful, funny, and kind. And having her around would stop you from flirting with Jessica's teacher."

Phil closed his eyes and sighed. "Mom."

Kara chuckled, but then her smile softened as she burped Mira. "I'm just teasing you. Mallory is wonderful, and she's great with Jessica. I can see how much they've connected. I'd like to see her stick around. That's all."

"That doesn't mean I have to adopt her."

"No, you don't." Kara heaved a breath, and Phil prepared himself for whatever button she intended to push next. "Speaking of adoption," she said, clearly changing the topic.

Phil moaned as he realized what she was getting at. "Oh, Mom."

"Lynn told us last night she wants us to keep Mira. Not that we were surprised."

Looking at her, the bloodshot eyes, the dark circles that now seemed permanent, and the way her hair was always swept up and out of the way, tugged at his heart. "You cannot adopt this baby. Look at you. You're exhausted."

"I'm exhausted because your father and I were up half the night talking about this."

"You're exhausted because for the last six months you've been responsible for caring for that kid day in and day out."

"Well, somebody has to be responsible for her." Though her voice was soft, gentle as to not upset the little one on her shoulder, her eyes and words spoke volumes. There was no debating this. She had the same fire in her eyes talking about Mira as she'd always had for Jessica. And before that, for Phil. She was a fierce protector, a mama bear in every sense of the term, and nothing Phil said would make her see that Mira was too much for them to handle. Even so, he had to try to talk some sense into her.

"Mom, there are plenty of families out there, good families, who would adopt her. It doesn't have to be you and Dad."

Kara nodded. "Yeah, and until one of those families is vetted and comes along, she'll be dropped into a foster home. You are perfectly aware how broken her little soul is already, Phil. That would cause her so much damage, damage that can be avoided. She has a home here. With us. Where she's been for the entirety of her very short life. This will just make it official."

"Officially *permanent*."

"I know what adoption means, Phil. Listen, this isn't just about what we can do for her. We need her, too. Harry wasn't there for you growing up. You have no idea how much guilt he still carries around. He hates the idea of letting Mira be raised by strangers. She's a part of this family now."

"Two things about that. First, it wasn't Dad's fault he wasn't there for me. Grandma Elaine never told him about me. Second thing? Adopting a baby won't change the past, but it will definitely change your future."

"Having Mira will give him back something that he lost."

"You're going to commit to a lifetime decision because Dad's parents were manipulative jerks thirty years ago?"

She resumed patting Mira's back when the baby squirmed. "We're going to commit to this child who has been in our home and our lives for months because she needs someone to love and protect her. Part of our decision was based on the fact that Harry missed out on something spectacular, and he knows that. Raising Mira won't be the same as raising you, but it will help us all in ways that we probably didn't even realize we needed. Harry isn't the only one who missed out, Phil. I never had an opportunity to grow as a parent with him. You never had an opportunity to be a big brother."

He raised his brows at her. Was she really going to try to make this about him? "The urge to torment a younger sibling has passed."

"Do you think Mira's urge to have an older brother protect her has passed?"

"I have a hard time thinking that she'd see me as an older brother when I could be her father. And seeing you as parents when you're..."

She raised her brows in warning. "If you call me old, I'll ground you."

He chuckled, having no doubt that she'd likely try. Harry would probably back her up, too. They really had become a team, a solid parental unit, even if it was three decades later than it should have been. He softened his smile. "I wasn't going to call you old, but I can't help but point out that you'll probably be the most *mature* parents at her high school graduation."

Kara laughed. "I think that's the first time you've ever referred to me as mature."

"Probably the last," he deadpanned.

"Just so you know, I'm not completely over the hill. My factory is still working. One mishap like the one your father and I had in high school, and you would be a *biological* big brother."

He cringed. "Mom. How many times do I have to tell you it is *not okay* to talk to me about your sex life?"

"She will know we aren't her birth parents," Kara continued as if he hadn't spoken. "I know this is all a bit unconventional, but when has this family followed the norm?"

Never. They'd never followed the norm. "Do you feel this is what is best for Mira?"

"This is already her home, Phil. We're already her family."

"What if Lynn changes her mind? What if she decides she doesn't want to give Mira up? That will hurt you so much, Mom."

She didn't deny his observation. The love she felt for that baby was so deep, it shined in her eyes whenever she looked at her. This was more than the care she'd taken with the other babies who had passed through her arms. Her connection to

Mira ran all the way to her soul, and Phil was terrified how much it would break her if she were to lose this child.

"We'll cross that bridge if we get to it," Kara said, dismissing his worry. "I can't let her turn this baby over to strangers. Mira needs to have a well-rounded support system growing up. We can give her that. Even if we are old."

Phil hated the burden his parents were taking on, but he wasn't surprised that they were willing to step up like this. He guessed the reason she felt so close to Mira was because the situation hit a bit too close to home. Her parents had turned her out, too. She always had a weakness for people who had been turned out.

"She's a lucky kid to have you guys raise her. She'll have an interesting life."

Kara put her hand to his face as she smiled. "Yes, she will. Now. About you and Mallory."

"For God's sake, Mother."

"Only halfway," Annie said as Mallory filled her coffee mug. "I'm sore from physical therapy. I'm having a hard time holding on to things. If I spill, I'd like to keep it minimal."

Mallory stopped pouring the hot brew and frowned at the reminder that something as simple as sipping coffee could still present a challenge for her mother. She'd jumped right in to help Marcus drive Annie to and from her appointments, but watching her mom struggle through the exercises hadn't been easy. Mallory had to fight the urge to do everything for her. *Here, Mom, let me lift that five-pound weight. Hey, I can help you fasten that button. You just sit back and relax and let me do everything.*

Annie would have killed her.

Once, right after Annie came home from the hospital, she was having a hard time using her fork at a family dinner. Mallory offered to feed her. Annie just about came unglued. Marcus sat Mallory down and reminded her they had to let Annie fight her way back on her own. Even so, Mallory wanted to make everything right for Annie. Maybe that was why Annie was so concerned about why she'd moved back home. One more person trying to coddle her.

Phil's advice had been wise, and Mallory was doing her best to heed it. She had to let Annie take care of herself. She'd ask if she needed help.

But that was so much easier said than done. She'd probably have to ask him to remind her of that every day until she finally got over the deep-seated need to rescue her mom.

Annie picked up the conversation where she'd left off as Mallory filled her own mug to near overflowing. "I'm not saying you should marry Phil."

Mallory nearly laughed but managed to keep her amusement to a sarcastic grin. "Well, that's good, because I've been back in town for like a month, and I'm not even dating anyone—

including Phil—so I'm fairly certain a marriage proposal isn't on his to-do list."

Annie ignored her as she focused on gripping the sugar scoop. "I'm just saying he is a great guy. Jessica is the sweetest little girl in the world."

"I know, Mom."

"I adore them both."

Mallory nodded, watching little white crystals fall off the scoop as Annie lifted it to her cup. "I can tell."

"You'd make a great family."

Jerking her focus from the spilled sugar, Mallory widened her eyes at her mother. "*What*? Where the *hell* is this coming from?"

Annie smiled widely. She even chuckled a little. "Annoying, isn't it?"

Grabbing a napkin, skipping over the Mom-can-do-that-herself step, Mallory cleaned up the mess. "You butting in on my nonexistent love life? A little bit, yeah."

Annie patted her hand. "Oh, honey, remember when I wasn't ready to date Marcus, but you just kept shoving how great he was down my throat? 'Mom, he's so sweet. Mom, he's so handsome. Mom, he's so in love with you. I never had a dad.' You actually said that. Remember?"

Mallory playfully glared at her. "Payback. Is that what this is?"

Instead of answering, Annie lifted her mug and blew on her coffee.

"The difference is Marcus was in love with you. Phil is just a friend." For some odd reason, saying that aloud made Mallory feel a little bit like someone had taken an ice pick to her heart. She didn't like the sound of that one bit, but it was the truth. "He's just a buddy. A pal," she said, more for her benefit than her mother's.

Annie eased her cup down and sat back. "Well, that's a shame. Your buddy, your pal, is one handsome little devil. He's smart and successful and a wonderful father. Somebody is going to snatch him up before you know it."

Mallory shook her head, probably far too vehemently. "He's not interested in dating, either."

Annie looked at her daughter and tilted her head. "So you've talked about dating?"

"Not each other. Jeez, Mom. If you must know, we talked about this." She gestured between the two of them. "You and Kara seem awfully determined to pair us up with each other or anyone else who comes along. Since when do you care if I date?"

"I care. I've always cared."

Mallory rolled her eyes. "Your sex talk was more along the lines of a Stephen King novel. You intentionally tried to traumatize me."

"You lie," Annie insisted. "I simply wanted you to know that most men are demons straight from hell."

"Most?"

"Some. But that's beside the point. Men do have their benefits. Just how good of *friends* are you?"

Mallory got that same icky feeling she'd felt when she'd caught Annie and Marcus kissing on the couch. Not because the thought of Phil being more than a friend was bad—not that they were more than friends, but if they were, it wouldn't necessarily be a bad thing—but since when did her mother ask questions like *that?* "*Whoa*. What?"

Annie laughed. "I'm just asking because Kara is really worried about Jessica. She's been making a lot of comments lately about her mother. Kara thinks she needs someone in her life, a mother figure."

"Isn't finding a mother for Jessica Phil's job?"

"Nobody is asking you to be her mother. You're too young for that. Being a mother sucks sometimes."

"Thanks. *Mom*."

"You may have blocked out your teenage years, but I remember them quite well," Annie said.

Mallory frowned, recalling some of her more rebellious moments—like coming home with a chunk of her head shaved. Her mother swore she could never spend the night at Cassie Richards's house again. "I haven't blocked out anything. You were just…mean."

Annie smiled but didn't counter her assessment. "Kara wants a support system for Jessica as she grows up."

"Again, isn't this Phil's job?"

"I'm worried for her, too. She's talked to me more than once about not having a mom. It bothers her. I'd like to see her have someone she can connect with. I saw the pictures of you guys yesterday, Mal. She was looking at you with pure adoration."

Mallory's heart swelled at her mother's observation. She'd been looking at Jess with pure adoration as well. She'd never connected with a kid on that level before, but she thought it was probably the most magical friendship she'd ever had. Jessica was so real, and honest, and full of love. She simply radiated that, and Mallory soaked it up.

Even so, this role her mother was creating wasn't Mallory's to fill. "I was dressed like a comic book character. A lot of kids looked at me like I was awesome."

"Mally," Annie said gently, using a nickname she saved for the most serious of conversations, "this was different, and you know it. She likes you. Really likes you. And you really like her. I can tell by the way you talk about her."

"I'm not denying that, Mom. I think she is a great little person, but I'm not exactly mom material. I'm just starting to figure out this adulthood thing. I have no business advising some mini-Phil on how to get through life. I like hanging out with her. I like hanging out with Phil. But if she needs a mom, her father needs to find someone who can do that for her. It's not me."

Annie sighed. "Okay."

Okay? Like that was ever the answer with her mother. "What?"

"Nothing."

"Oh, please, Mom. You had that whole disappointed look

thing that you get."

"I did not."

Mallory tilted her head in the same way Annie did when silently pressing for the truth.

Annie pressed her lips together, apparently debating what to say. Grabbing Mallory's hand, she stared into her eyes. "Jessica needs someone to do things like dress her up as a pony and help her with her makeup."

"She's eleven," Mallory countered. "She doesn't wear makeup yet."

"Would Phil have taken her to that convention dressed like a pink horse if you hadn't invited them?"

Mallory laughed. "God, no."

"Neither would Kara or Harry. But she loved it, didn't she?"

Oh, maternal guilt. Mallory had actually forgotten how good Annie could be at this. "Yes. She loved every moment of it."

"And so did you, right?"

"I did."

Annie shrugged. "So. She needs more of that in her life. She needs more of *you* in her life. That's all I'm saying."

"No, that's not all you're saying. You said she needs a mother figure."

"Friend. She needs a friend."

"I don't mind being her friend, but don't try to force me into a role that isn't mine to fill. Even if I wanted to be a mother to her, I can't just decide that. She has a parent. A father. That's his responsibility. Not yours, not mine, and not Kara's. No matter how well-intentioned any of us might be."

"Phil is stubborn. He won't see what he doesn't want to see."

Mallory frowned. As if her mother had any room to talk about someone being stubborn.

Annie lifted her hands. "Okay. Just consider one other thing and I'll let it go."

"Yeah, right."

Annie lowered her voice in the way she did to make certain Mallory listened. "She needs someone like you needed Marcus. I couldn't see it because I chose not to. I chose to believe what I gave you was enough because it was all I had to give. When I got hurt, even though you were an adult and you had uncles and friends who loved you, you needed someone to fill that role that was missing your entire life. You needed someone to be a father to you. Thankfully you had Marcus. He was right there, giving you that paternal love that you'd never had. Supporting you like a father would do. He's done that for you."

Mallory swallowed hard, remembering how many nights she'd counted on Marcus to get her through when Annie was in a coma and recovering from her injury. Even now she needed that man to make her believe things were going to be okay. "Yes, he has. He has been an amazing surrogate father to me."

"So who's going to do that for Jessica? If Phil isn't interested in dating, the chances of him finding someone who will accept and help Jess grow up are slim to none, wouldn't you say? She's getting older, and at some point, she's going to have questions and problems and issues that he can't help her with. Who is going to help her, Mallory?"

Sitting back, Mallory frowned. "When the hell did you become so emotionally manipulative?"

Annie smiled as she tapped her forehead. "I have brain damage now. I can't always control myself."

The self-satisfied smile on her lips told Mallory she knew exactly what she was doing.

CHAPTER SEVEN

*M*allory watched Jessica run along the lake's shoreline before focusing on the way-too-quiet man walking next to her. After a spontaneous lunch of sandwiches at a local sub shop, they'd decided the day was too nice to let pass by. Actually, she and Jessica had decided that. Phil had seemed distracted ever since she arrived at his house. They were supposed to start binge-watching *Doctor Who*, but Jessica insisted she was starving, and Phil said they hadn't gone to the grocery store yet.

That didn't seem to bother Jessica much at all. She was pretty eager to get out and have lunch at a restaurant. She seemed to enjoy the culinary arts...or at least the eating part...as much as Mal did. They'd made a pact to get two different sandwiches and split them. As they'd had a serious debate over their options, Phil seemed like he couldn't care less.

As they ate, critiquing their selections like a Food Network star might, Phil had sat quietly. He was definitely rolling something around in his mind.

When Jessica was far enough ahead on the beach, Mallory gently bumped into him. "Spit it out. What's bothering you?"

Phil shoved his hands in his pants pockets and hesitated before answering, as if considering what to say. "I stopped by to see my parents this morning. They're going to try to adopt Mira. Her mom has realized dropping by to check in on occasion isn't exactly being a good mother. Apparently walking away from her daughter is a better option."

Mallory exhaled slowly. "Wow. I'll never get these parents who just ditch their kids."

"Yeah." He frowned. "Me either."

She hesitated. "I'm sorry. I know Jessica's mom bailed, so this probably stings you a bit more than most."

"Katrina wasn't any more maternal than Mira's mom. Some women simply aren't meant to be mothers."

Mallory looked out at the sun reflecting off the calm surface of the lake. "Then we have men like my biological father. Whoever and wherever he is. There's a whole lot of parental dysfunction around here." She glanced at him when he didn't respond. She hoped she hadn't offended him. Harry hadn't been around for Phil, either, but that wasn't by choice. That was because of an entirely different set of circumstances. "How do you feel about your parents adopting?" she asked, hoping to move the topic to something less personally painful for both of them.

He lifted his shoulders and let them fall casually. "It's their choice."

"Come on. Don't give me that passive bullshit. You don't look happy."

Phil looked out over the lake. The water was flat, despite Jessica tossing rock after rock into it. She was supposed to be collecting them for a class project, but she was obviously far more interested in seeing how far she could send them.

"I'm worried that they're taking on more than they can handle," Phil said. "They've just gotten settled into a life together. Their marriage is going to be completely disrupted."

She bit her lip for a moment, carefully considering his words. "Are your parents having problems?"

"Hmm?" He creased his brow at her, but then he must have realized how his concern had come across. "Oh, no. Nothing like that. They're very happy from what I can tell."

"Well, your mom is a midwife, and she's already raised you. She knows what she's getting into by taking on a baby."

"But Dad doesn't. He had a few stepkids from his first marriage, but they were older when he married their mom. Once they were divorced, he didn't have much contact with them. He didn't come back into the picture until I was an adult. He's never had an infant full-time without any breaks. I'm not sure he knows what he's getting into."

"I doubt he's as oblivious as you seem to think, Phil. For as long as I've known your parents, they've had infants tucked under their wings. They've had babies in and out of their house since they've been married. It's kind of their thing. Some people foster kittens. Your parents foster struggling single mothers."

"That's not the same as having a kid twenty-four-seven."

"But it's a pretty good indicator of what's to come. What are you really worried about?"

"It's just..." He looked away from her, back out to the water. "All of this talk about how Mira needs a solid family structure... Mom's right. Jessica needs someone else in her life. I listened to her talking about all the reasons she should adopt Mira, and each one hit a nerve. Every kid needs the best chance possible to grow up strong and independent and well-rounded. Maybe I am denying Jessica that chance by not having someone in her life to fill the void Katrina left."

Mallory moaned and rolled her head back. "Oh, man. I thought it was just my mother."

"What?"

She shook her head and started walking again, taking slightly longer strides to close some of the distance between them and Jessica. "You aren't the only one who had an interesting parental visit this morning. My mom is all about how Jess needs a woman in her life to help her out."

"Why would your mom... Oh, right. I'm sure Jessica has talked about this with Annie."

Mal nodded. "She sure has. And Mom thinks that by dressing her up like a pony, I've proven I'm the one. Sorry. I'm not butting in on this dilemma of yours. I just didn't realize Jessica's lack of a mother was a universal conversation. Honestly, I thought Mom was overstepping. So this pool that our parents are tossing us into isn't just about us, then?"

"Guess not."

She looked up at him, and their gazes locked. Her heart did that funny little flip thing she seemed to be feeling more and more these days. Something strange was going on inside of her, and she didn't particularly care for it. Instead of listening to instinct and moving closer to him, she looked at Jessica farther down the beach. "I'm here for Jess if she needs anything. She's helped my mom in ways nobody else could. I know she's just a kid, but she understood what Mom was going through when she got home from the hospital, and Mom needed that. I'm more than happy to return the favor. If she ever needs anyone to talk to about...*whatever*...I'm happy to listen."

"Really? You wouldn't mind?"

"Not at all. That girl's a hoot."

He laughed softly. "Yeah, she is."

"Don't feel like you need someone in your life just so Jess can have someone in hers. I'm happy to walk her through her teenage angst."

"That'd be great." His smile softened as he looked at her. "Thanks, Mal."

Mallory couldn't quite explain the level of relief she felt. Somehow, the idea of someone else being that person for Jessica didn't sit right with her. She didn't want to trust someone else with molding that girl's mind. If anyone was going to teach her about boys and clothes and makeup, Mallory wanted to be the one. She felt she should be the one. After all, who else was going to go to comic book conventions with her?

"Dad!" Jessica screamed, breaking through the serenity of the moment. "Come quick!"

The conversation ended as they rushed to see what had Jessica so panicked. Mallory gasped as she came upon a dog lying on its side in the rocks, panting heavily, its eyes wide as it looked at them.

"Look at his leg. He's hurt," Jess pointed out.

The dog whimpered, as if to confirm her assessment. Fur from his back hip had been stripped, exposing bloody skin. The leg was lying in way that was clearly indicating the bone had been broken.

"Stay back," Phil warned. "Jessica, keep back."

Mallory pulled Jess against her as Phil slowly approached the dog. If the animal attacked, she was more than ready to get between it and Jessica. Her heart raced at the thought of Jessica getting hurt. Her instinct told her to leave the animal, call someone to check on it, just in case, but her heart broke as the dog whined again.

"Hey, buddy," Phil said gently as he crouched down.

"Strange dogs might bite, Daddy," Jess warned.

"I'm being careful, Punk." He slowly extended his hand. The dog made a sad sound as it lifted its head. "What happened to you?" He moved his hand along the dog's long black body until the animal yelped. Looking over his shoulder, he said, "Mal, there's a blanket in my trunk. Go grab it."

"What's wrong?"

Phil returned his attention to the mutt. "I think he got hit by a car."

Jessica gasped dramatically. "Oh, no!"

"We'll find a vet to take a look at him." Phil tossed his keys to Mallory.

"Then can we take him home?" Jess asked.

"No," Phil said without thinking twice.

Mallory didn't mean to, but she pouted right along with Jessica. "Who will look after him if we don't take him?"

"Yeah, Daddy," Jessica chimed in. "Who will take care of him?"

Phil frowned at both of them. "He probably has a family. We'll take him to the vet. They'll find out who he belongs to."

"Look how skinny he is." Mal pointed to his visible ribcage. "He's a stray."

"Daddy," Jess said in a soft, almost pleading voice, "what would Grandma do?"

Mallory tried not to laugh, but a burst of a giggle escaped before she was able to swallow it down.

"Grandma never leaves a stray behind," Phil mumbled. "Go get the blanket, Mal. We'll see what the vet says."

Mallory leaned down and looked in Jessica's eyes. "You stay back, okay. He seems nice now, but he still might be mean. Let Daddy take care of him, okay?"

"Okay," she said with whispered seriousness.

"Don't move unless Daddy tells you."

"I won't."

Mallory rushed off, trotting toward where Phil had parked farther down the lakeside. She was breathless by the time she reached the trunk. She had to chuckle as she moved aside a pink gymnastics bag and a glittery tutu. Nobody could ever say that he didn't let his kiddo try everything her heart desired. Some things seemed to stick more than others, but Mallory guessed that was pretty normal for kids Jessica's age.

The more time she spent with Phil and Jessica, the more she realized Phil had been right. Not just about Jessica not letting her disabilities get in her way but that Mallory couldn't get in the way of Annie learning to live with her disabilities. Who would have guessed that those two would have so much to teach and show her? She would be forever grateful to them for helping her learn how to not turn into an overbearing daughter.

As she ran back to the duo, blanket in hand, she was struck by something else. Jessica stood right where Mallory had left her, and relief washed over her. Somehow, she'd feared she'd come back to some horrific scene where the dog had just been waiting for her to turn her back before attacking. He hadn't. Jessica stood, still as could be, as Phil talked on his phone.

"He called a vet," Jessica said in a hushed voice as Mallory rejoined them.

Phil ended the call and accepted the blanket from Mallory's outstretched hand. He rested his elbows on his knees as he looked up at her. "All right. Here's the plan. You take Jess to the car and park it right over there." He pointed to the road that curved in close to the lake.

Mallory guessed the dog had been hit near that curve. Based on his extensive injuries, he couldn't have walked far.

"You drive," he said to Mallory then looked at Jessica. "You get in the passenger seat. I'll sit in back with this guy. We're going to take him to the vet and leave him. Got it?" He eyed them both. "We're leaving him."

Mallory swallowed the urge to argue. Taking Jessica's hand, she pulled her along before she could argue, either.

sh

"I can't believe I agreed to this," Phil said as Jessica tucked a blanket around the dog they'd rescued.

Mallory smiled without a bit of shame for her part in convincing him to bring the mutt home. "Look how happy she is."

He couldn't argue that point. Jessica had hushed and cooed and whispered to the dog from the moment the vet released his patient. Much like she'd learned from her grandmother, Jessica petted and hummed to soothe the stray. "She's wanted a pet for as long as I can remember."

"Well, this guy needed a home, and he's so sweet."

"For now. What happens when his cast comes off and he can actually move around?"

Mallory eyed the dog. "I think if he were aggressive, he

would have shown it by now. Even the vet said he was a good dog." She sat on the couch next to him and watched just as closely as Jessica kissed the black head she'd been patting. She might not say it, but she was feeling protective, ready to intervene in a moment's notice if needed. She'd been that way ever since they'd picked up the damn dog. She might be trying to convince him that the dog wasn't mean, but she hadn't stopped anticipating his every move.

Phil agreed with her assessment. If the dog were aggressive, it would have shown by now. He'd been put through quite a bit since they'd found him by the lake. Even when he was broken and raw, he let Phil pick him up and carry him without so much as a few whines and whimpers. The entire trip to the vet had been him looking up with thankful eyes, not a bit of hesitation or suspicion to be seen. Simple, pure gratitude.

He tried to focus on the dog and not notice how close Mallory was, but with every passing second his comfort with the stray grew and he was able to focus on something else. Like the woman sitting next to him. "I'm turning into my mother."

"Hardly." She laughed. "Taking in a stray dog is a far cry from adopting a baby."

"Shh." He glanced at Jess before whispering, "I'm not telling her about Mira until everything is finalized."

Mallory put her fingertips to her lips. "Sorry."

"I just don't want her to get excited about the idea in case the adoption falls through."

"That makes sense." She watched Jessica for a moment before

tilting her chin so she could eye him. "Do you think it will? Do you really think she'll back out?"

"Who knows. Lynn—Mira's mother—isn't exactly known for her reliability. She could be feeling this way now, but the reality of giving up her baby could change her mind. That's a big decision."

"Did, um, did Katrina give up her rights or did she just leave?"

"Oh, no. My mom had seen that type of situation more than once. She was on top of it. We had an attorney about five minutes after Katrina left the hospital. As wonderful and sweet as my mother can be, she does not mess around when it comes to her tribe. Our attorney tracked Katrina down with paperwork in hand. Her options were to foot her share of the medical bills or sign the papers. Just like that, she gave up her rights, my name, our marriage, our life. Everything. She walked away like we never happened."

Mallory put her hand on his and squeezed it gently. "I'm so sorry. It should never be that easy for a mother, or a wife, to walk away." Looking at Jessica, she shook her head. "Who could give up on that sweet angel?"

Phil stared at where Mallory was touching him until she pulled away. "I think that was part of the reason we stayed in Seattle as long as we did. Part of me was hoping she'd come back. Not for me." He nodded toward his daughter. "For her. I get why Katrina left. It was hell not knowing if Jess was going to live through her surgery. Raising her has had certain challenges that most parents probably don't face. So I do understand why she left. I just don't understand how she could stay away forever."

Mallory shrugged and sat back, apparently accepting that Jessica was safe with the dog. "My dad isn't even listed on my birth certificate. That space is just blank. I know his name is Steve Riley, but I never met him. I thought about looking him up, but Mom swears we were better off, and I believe her. If he'd been worth a damn, he wouldn't have run away when Mom told him about me. And if he wanted to find me, he could have. I was born right here in Stonehill where my family has always lived. Mom's full name is on her business, and her shooting was all over the news last year. If he wanted to find me, he could. Clearly he doesn't."

Phil grabbed her hand, just as she'd done to his, only he didn't squeeze and let go. He held her hand intentionally. "That's his loss, Mal. Not yours."

She nodded. "And not being here for Jess is Katrina's loss. Not Jessica's. Look at her. She's like the dog whisperer."

He smiled as the pup sighed with what could only be described as contentment as Jessica pulled the blanket around him and promised he was going to be okay. He started to remind his daughter not to put her face next to the dog's, but when she planted a kiss on the black head, she received a lick in return and a beaming smile broke on her face. "They're going to be inseparable, aren't they?"

"I think so."

He rubbed his thumb over Mallory's hand. He wasn't flirting

exactly, but he felt connected to her in that moment and was determined to stay connected. When she tightened her hand in his, his heart sang and any hesitation he might have had at keeping the dog was gone. That had nothing to do with the dog and everything to do with how this moment—he and Mallory watching Jess with their new pet—seemed to be everything he'd ever missed out on. "Have you decided on his name, Jess?"

She finally tore her attention from the dog and looked at Phil. "I think we should call him Lucky. Don't you?"

"I think that's perfect."

"I had a rabbit named Lucky when I was a kid," Mallory offered. "Of course, that was for a different reason."

"Because rabbit's feet are lucky," Jessica said.

"Exactly."

Phil didn't want to break up the unexpected normalcy he was feeling, but his watch vibrated as the hour changed, and he realized how late it was getting. "It's time to say good night to Lucky, Punk."

"*Dad*," Jessica whined dramatically. "He'll be lonely if I leave him."

Regretfully, he took his hand from Mallory's and pushed himself up. "He'll be fine."

Jessica turned to Mallory, clearly seeking support, but Mallory just lifted her hands helplessly. "You can't stay up with him all night."

Jess stuck her lip out a bit but kissed her new best friend's head once again and stood. "Sleep tight, Lucky." She hugged Phil but then shocked him by walking to the couch and throwing her arms around Mallory's neck. "Night, Mal. Take care of Lucky for me, okay?"

Mallory hugged her tight. "I will. Night, Jess."

"Thanks for taking me to the lake today and for staying with us at the vet's office and for helping us buy stuff for Lucky. I'm glad you were there today."

"Me, too."

"I'll be right back," Phil said to Mallory. He followed Jessica toward her bedroom. "Teeth brushed, hair brushed, jammies on, and in bed in ten minutes."

"I know, Dad," she said with the same exasperated tone she used every night these days. She used to get upset if he didn't follow her around, telling her what to do. Now she seemed to have no use for his reminders. Leaning on her bedroom doorjamb, he watched her open one of her dresser drawers and pull out a nightgown. "Stop growing up so fast, Punk."

She turned back to him, her face dead serious. "I can't control how fast I grow."

"Well, try." He crossed the room and put a kiss on her forehead. "See you in the morning."

"Is Mallory going home?" she asked before he reached the bedroom door.

He turned to face her. "She'll go home sometime. Why?"

"She said she'd look after Lucky."

"He doesn't need someone to watch him all night. He's gotta get some sleep, too."

"Will you sleep on the couch so you'll hear him if he needs help?"

He started to argue, but he actually could see her logic. The last thing he wanted was for the new dog to pee in the house. Considering the dog was obviously a stray, Phil doubted he was potty-trained. "Yeah. I'll sleep on the couch. Night, Punk."

"Do you like her?" she called before he could leave.

Biting his lip, he turned, frustrated that she was keeping him from returning to Mallory. "The dog?"

"Lucky is a boy," Jessica reminded him. "I mean Mallory. Do you like *Mallory*?"

He nodded. "She's nice."

Jessica frowned at him as if he were the one being difficult. "But do you *like* her, Daddy?"

Oh, crap. Here we go. Stepping back into her bedroom so Mallory didn't overhear, he said, "She's my friend, Jess. Just like she's your friend."

"That's all?"

"Yeah. That's all."

"I saw you holding hands on the couch."

"Friends can hold hands."

She dropped her shoulders, looking like he'd just stomped on all her hopes and dreams. "What's wrong with her?"

He laughed softly at her posture. She appeared to be completely fed up with him. "Nothing."

"Then why don't you *like* her?"

"I haven't known her very long, Jessica."

"That's not true. We met her when Dianna and Paul got married forever ago. Dianna is Grandma's best friend in the whole world, and Paul is Mallory's uncle. We were at the wedding. You talked to her. Remember?"

Yes, he remembered too well. Mallory had been wearing a bright blue dress that most people probably would have frowned upon at a wedding, but Mal always seemed to wear bright clothes. It hadn't taken long for Phil to realize how much that reflected her personality. Bright. Bold. Strong. She stood out to him for so many reasons, at the wedding and now. But this was the exact thing he'd been concerned about, something he should have considered when he'd sat on the couch holding Mallory's hand.

In the moment, that had felt so right to him, but the signals it sent to Jessica were too confusing.

"Yes, Jessica. I talked to her, but I didn't really *know* her. We just were nice to each other. I'm getting to know her now. And we're *friends* now."

She shoved her dresser drawer shut harder than necessary. "Well, *I* like her."

He crossed the room and sat on her bed. Resting his elbows on his knees, he sighed and ran his hands over his face. "Listen, kiddo, I know you've been feeling like there's a hole in our lives. All your friends have moms who do stuff with them and teach them things that I don't know a lot about, but we can't just decide that we like Mallory and keep her like we're going to keep

Lucky. I know you want a mom. I get that. I understand it more than you know."

"Because you didn't have a dad."

He nodded. "But before I let someone even think about getting close to you like that, I need to know that she's the right person for you *and* for me. That takes time. It takes a long time to know if you love someone enough to marry them and even more time before you know if they are going to be a good parent to your kid. I'm not going to let just anybody into our lives, Jessica. Not like that."

"Mallory isn't just anybody. She's Annie's daughter and my friend."

"I know. And she's a good friend, too. But that doesn't mean she'd be good at being your mom. You know what she said today? She said if you ever need anything you can talk to her. She said she'd be your friend, no matter what."

"That's not the same," Jess whispered as a sheen covered her eyes.

Phil's heart broke at the disappointment on her face. "I know, Punk. But it's the best I can do right now."

She looked disheartened, but it really was the best he could do. Standing, he kissed her head. "Night, babe."

"Night, Daddy." Her tone was pouty, confirming she wasn't happy with his answer, but he opted not to further the discussion.

Mallory was sitting in the spot Jessica had vacated, petting the dog's head. "You're going to be spoiled rotten. You know that, right?"

"By me or Jessica?"

She rolled her head up as she realized he'd returned. "By the entire Martinson-Canton clan, I suspect."

Phil shrugged. "I'm sure he will be. Wanna hang out for a while? We never got started on our marathon."

"It's closing in on nine thirty."

"You have a curfew, Mal?"

"No, but I assumed you had a strict schedule. Up at six. Work by eight. Home by six. Dinner by seven. Bed by ten." She made a show of looking at her phone. "It's now 9:22. Getting late, Dad."

He creased his brow, again feeling that strange sense of hurt that she didn't seem to know he had a lighter side. That was the same sting he'd felt at the convention. "I'll have you know that just last night, I stayed up until after eleven."

"Party animal." Standing, she brushed her hands together. "Actually, it is a work night for both of us. I should go. We'll start that marathon another time."

"Sounds like a plan." Standing back, he had a sudden rush of awkwardness that he'd never felt when Mallory was gathering her things to leave. Something seemed to be urging him toward her, pleading with him to not let her leave. As she grabbed her coat from the hook by the wall, his breath quickened. He was running out of time to stop her, but what reason could she possibly have to stay?

He'd told Jessica he didn't like Mallory, but that hadn't been the entire truth. He'd known it when he said it, but he had to be very careful of the ideas that were put into his daughter's head. She clung to things, got attached, and didn't always understand when plans had to change. He couldn't imagine how hard she'd take it if he and Mallory started dating and then decided they weren't compatible. Jessica would be so disappointed. So would Phil, so it would be best not to even think about that until he was absolutely certain that was the best next step.

But this uneasiness in his stomach didn't seem to want to listen to his excuses. His racing heart didn't seem to want to listen to his warnings.

Mallory stuck her feet in her shoes, rocking them back and forth as she shoved instead of simply untying the laces, and looked up at him. She was going to say something, but the words seemed to leave her. Her cheeks flushed bright pink, her mouth hung open, and her eyes locked on his.

Phil swallowed hard and took a step forward without thinking. He put his hands to her face, and her eyes widened. One more deep breath, and he pressed his mouth to hers before he lost his courage.

She froze like that princess in the movie about the ice queen that Jessica had finally stopped watching on a never-ending loop. Like a wet shirt hung on a line in the middle of winter. Like a woman who wasn't expecting or wanting to be kissed.

Oh. Crap.

That was not the reaction he was hoping to get. Leaning back, he fumbled for the words to apologize as she stared up at him with wide, light gray eyes. Before his apology formed, however, she leaned up and her mouth was on his. He felt the same shock that she must have, the same surprise that had her standing as still as an ice statue. He got over his shock quickly, though.

Holding her soft cheeks in his palms, he returned her kiss. Sweet, tender, and warm. Just like her.

The moment didn't last nearly as long as he would have liked, but when she pulled back, instead of looking wide-eyed and shocked, she was smiling. "I could stay," she whispered but then closed her eyes and gave her head a hard shake. "No. I can't. I can't. I really have to go." She heaved a breath as she peered up at him with a plea in her eyes, looking absolutely torn. "Tell me I have to go."

He didn't want to, but that was for the best. Jessica could get up and down a dozen times on a good night. Knowing Lucky was in the other room, Phil expected her excuses to get out of bed would double, if not triple. If Mallory stayed, his insistence that they were just friends would likely be blown out of the water. Jessica had already seen them holding hands. He couldn't imagine the idea she'd get if she caught them kissing.

Brushing his hand over Mallory's hair, he forced himself to stand by the decision. "You have to go."

"*Before* I do something bad?"

Phil chuckled as her impish grin spread and she batted her long lashes. "Yes. Before *we* do something bad."

She pouted in the most seductive way. "Perhaps we can plan that for another night."

Heat filled his cheeks. He wasn't usually one to blush, but something in her voice told him things had definitely just changed for the better. "Go home, Mallory."

She lifted her bag over her shoulder and took a step back but then fisted his shirt and pulled him to her. One big step, and she put her lips to his. Her tongue lightly brushed over his lip, sending a tsunami of heat to his core. So many promises in that one swift motion. So much temptation he wanted to cry.

"Good night," she breathed, and then she was gone, and he was left with a giant smile, a racing heart, and an imagination gone absolutely insane.

CHAPTER EIGHT

*M*allory couldn't sleep all night. She couldn't stop thinking about how Phil had kissed her. Out of the blue, without the slightest bit of warning. She also couldn't stop obsessing about how she'd stood there like an idiot. She hadn't realized how much she'd wanted him to kiss her until he had, but she'd gone rigid like a deer in a spotlight. She guessed she had looked like one, too.

Poor guy had started to stutter, probably about to beg for her forgiveness, before her brain started working and she could stop thinking *he kissed me!* on a loop in her head. She hadn't exactly fantasized about Phil kissing her, but if she had, it wouldn't have played out with her acting like a mannequin for the first few seconds.

Once her brain snapped to and she was able to kiss him back, she'd damn near swooned. The innocence on his face, the questions in his eyes, had made her insides melt. She wished she had a picture of that moment. She imagined they would have looked like a pair of fools to anyone else. She wouldn't say their first kisses were wasted, but they certainly could have been sexier.

She'd remedy that. And the sooner the better.

She'd rushed through getting ready for work, looking at her watch over and over until she knew he was up and had Jessica off to school. Then she debated whether she should call him. She wanted to call him. She wanted to hear his voice, but she didn't want to seem desperate.

That didn't stop her, though. She called his cell as soon as she got behind the wheel of her car. Her smile spread so far it hurt when his voice filtered through her speakers. "Sorry to call so early," she said, even though she wasn't.

"No problem."

She took a breath. "What are you doing for dinner tonight?"

"Jess has gymnastics. I usually take her for nuggets after."

Her smile faded. "Oh."

"Why? What's up?"

"I was...well..." Straightening in her seat, she tapped into the strong, independent woman her mother had taught her to be. Taking a breath, she blurted out her intentions before she could second-guess herself. "I thought maybe we'd have dinner. Uh...just *us*."

"I, um..."

She swallowed at the hesitation in his voice. Oh, man. If he backtracked on their quick good-night, she was going to die of embarrassment. She'd all but offered to stay and "be bad." What the hell had she been thinking? Oh, right. She hadn't been thinking. Her head had started spinning, and her body had come alive and begged for more of whatever he offered.

The implication of them going on a date hung in her car like the scent of a flower.

"That'd be great," Phil finally said. "I, um, I would like that very much." His voice sounded unsure, but she decided that was probably just him being surprised. He probably hadn't seen that bold move coming. "I'll ask Dad if he can take Jess tonight."

"Well, if you don't want to add to what Harry and Kara already have on their plate, I'm sure Mom and Marcus would take her. Mom would love to see her showing off at class."

"That'd be great. If they can't, let me know, and I'll talk to my dad."

"Phil?"

"Hmm?"

"I just want to be clear: I *am* asking you out on a date."

He was quiet for a moment. "I haven't been on a date in a long time."

"Me either."

"I'll, um"—his voice sounded light, as if he were smiling in that way that made his cheek dimple—"I'll try to remember proper protocol."

She laughed. "As far as I'm concerned, proper protocol is *show up on time and be nice*."

"Well, even I can't mess that up too much. Let me know what your parents say about Jess, okay?"

"Will do." She ended the call and squealed, actually freaking squealed. She and Phil were going on a date. A real date. Not a take-Jess-to-do-something outing. A date. Like grown-ups. She tried to take her excitement down a notch, but as soon as she was at the office, she headed straight for the office Annie and Marcus shared. The space used to just be Annie's. Since her injury impacted not only her speech but her ability to drive, she couldn't meet clients any longer. They would have too hard a time understanding her. Since she was no longer an agent, it made more sense for Marcus to occupy the big space; however, there was a second desk that Annie utilized a few hours a week to contribute however she could. Today, she was hovering over her touchscreen laptop, frowning at something.

"A little early to look so frustrated," Mallory observed.

"Oh, it's never too early for that," Annie said. "How are you this morning?"

"Wonderful."

Lifting her brows, Annie sat back and focused on Mallory. "Oh? Does your good mood have anything to do with Phil Martinson-Canton?"

Mal narrowed her eyes. "Do you think, just once, you could contain your know-it-all shitshow?"

Marcus snickered as he slid by Mallory with two cups of coffee in his hands. "Fat chance."

"Hey," Annie chastised. "Mind your manners."

He kissed her head as he put a mug on her desk. "I was."

Returning her attention to Mallory, Annie chuckled. "Why are you feeling so wonderful this morning?"

"Because..." She grinned. "I asked Phil out on a date, and he said yes."

Annie gasped as she perked up. "Really?"

"The catch is Jessica has gymnastics tonight. I was hoping you guys would be able to take her so I can steal her father."

"Of course," Annie said without hesitation or checking with Marcus, who would be the one driving them around. "She can spend the night. We can take her to school in the morning." Finally, she looked at her husband. "Right?"

"Slow down," Mallory stated. "Jeez, Mom. We're just going out for dinner."

"No dessert, then?" Marcus grinned, and Annie chuckled.

"Why do you two make me regret everything I say to you?"

"Because we can, sweetie," Annie stated.

Mallory rolled her eyes but decided to move on. "What had you looking so frustrated when I came in?"

"Trying to update the newsletter template. I'm bored with the old one."

"Well. You do know that I'm a graphic designer, right? I'm sure I could figure something out."

Annie lowered her gaze to the screen, looking a bit defeated. "I know. Why don't you do it? I'm making more of a mess than anything."

Mallory's good mood dipped right along with her mother's.

Annie's contributions were limited enough, and here Mallory was taking away another one. "We should work on it together, Mom. I think my morning is pretty open. Shall we convene in the conference room with coffee and bagels?"

Her smile returned. "Sounds fun."

"See you there." She pushed herself off the door and went to her office, where she immediately called Phil. She was disappointed to get his voice mail but happy to leave news that Annie and Marcus were on board for gymnastics class. She glanced at her door, making sure her nosy mother wasn't eavesdropping. "Let me know when they need to pick her up. Or if you want us to drop her off or...whatever. Also, I thought I should warn you that I'll probably still find a way to talk about comic books and anime. I don't want you think that I'm suddenly going to turn into a mature human being just because there isn't a kid around."

Ending the call, she bit her lip to try to stop her smile from breaking her face.

"Ready?" Annie asked from the doorway, her smile almost as big as Mallory's.

Oh, man. This was going to be interesting. She'd have to use all her superpowers to keep Annie focused on the newsletter instead of her and Phil. She wasn't sure her powers were strong enough. Taking her laptop with her, she went to the break room, filled a mug with coffee, and dropped a plain bagel onto a plate. Juggling her load, she went to the conference room, where Annie was waiting for her.

"Okay," Mal said, opening her laptop. "What are you thinking for the newsletter?" When Annie didn't answer, she chuckled. "It's just a date, Mom. Stop planning my wedding."

Annie nudged her. "It's not that."

She glanced at her and lifted her brows to express her disbelief. "Then what is it?"

"All I've ever wanted was to see that smile on your face. It's been too long, Mal."

A spear went through her heart. "Mom."

Stroking her hand over Mallory's hair, Annie sniffled. "I know you gave up everything you ever wanted in California to take care of me. You can deny it all you want, but I know. I love you for it, but that's not what I wanted for you. I want you to be happy. You look happy this morning."

"I am," Mal whispered. "I like him."

"Good."

"But slow your roll, Mom. It's *one* date."

Wrapping her arm around Mallory's shoulders, Annie hugged her and kissed her head. "For now."

"Mom," she moaned but couldn't help her smile from spreading again. "You're impossible."

Phil chuckled when he realized his stomach was fluttering as he walked to Mallory's door. He'd dropped Jessica off, decked out in her pink leotard and sweatpants, and had rushed off to pick up his date. His *date*. The word had made him smile like a fool all damned day.

Knocking on Mal's door, he let out a long, nervous breath. No, not nervous. *Eager*. Excited. Over the flippin' moon.

She opened her door, and his heart leaped. She wasn't wearing anything fancier than he'd ever seen before. They'd hung out after work plenty of times, but her tight, mid-thigh-length white skirt and fitted lavender blouse seemed to be as sexy as any lingerie he'd ever seen. Her hair had waves styled throughout. Again, nothing he hadn't seen on her before, but tonight they seemed to be begging for him to run his fingers through them.

And her purple-painted lips? Had they always been so damned inviting?

She stepped aside and gestured for him to enter. He was tempted to stay on her porch. Somehow that seemed like the gentlemanly thing to do, but the soft scent of her flowery body spray lured him in.

"I just need to grab a sweater. I always get cold in restaurants."

He knew that about her. Almost every time they ate out, halfway through she'd slip her arms into a sweater or a coat to warm up. More than once he'd pointed out that if she dressed a bit warmer than her usual T-shirts or thin blouses, she'd stay warmer. She'd just roll her eyes and tell him he sounded like her mother.

"Have you picked a restaurant?" she asked.

"You should pick."

With her sweater draped over her forearm, she grinned. "But I asked *you* out, so *you* should pick."

"Mexican."

She crinkled her nose. "You should pick something other than Mexican."

"That little Italian place on the square is good."

Her pursed lips let him know she didn't agree.

Laughing, he shrugged. "Why don't you pick?"

She started for the door but stopped right in front of him. Inches from him. The teasing in her eyes faded as she blatantly skimmed her eyes over his face. The air between them shifted from teasing to tense—a good kind of tension.

"Maybe," she whispered, "we should just order something for delivery."

"We could do that," he agreed. Sliding his arm around her lower back and digging the fingers of his other hand into her hair, he pulled her to him. With no air of pretense, he claimed her mouth and she claimed his. This was much better than their first attempt at kissing. This mutual meeting of passionate lips sent heat straight through him, and the deep moan that vibrated up her throat and into his mouth told him she was just as pleased.

"Take your coat off," she said breathlessly when their lips parted. "Stay a while."

His coat fell in a lump of black fleece around their feet. He ignored it as he pulled her to him again, this time using his hands on her hips to steer her toward the sofa. She fisted his shirt as she eased down, pulling him with her until he was stretched over her while she sank into the soft cushions. Holy hell. Looking down into her eyes, he was planning to tell her he had no expectations of intimacy if she wasn't ready, but the desire in her gaze stopped his words before they started.

She obviously wanted him just as much. His body lit on fire, an inferno that only this woman could put out but one that he hoped she never did. He wanted to burn like this for her forever. He suspected he would.

Lifting her head, she caught his mouth again, sliding her tongue between his lips and drawing him in with the taste of strawberries. He guessed it was the flavored water she liked to drink, but in that moment it was everything he'd come to expect from her.

Sweet. Tempting. Captivating.

He couldn't stop dipping his tongue in, demanding more. Running his hand down her side, he nearly melted into her when his palm found the soft skin of her thigh where her skirt had ridden up.

She pressed her hands against his chest as she struggled to release the buttons of his shirt. He didn't want to break their heated kiss, but he leaned back and undid the first two buttons so he could tug it over his head and toss it aside. She gripped his sides, pulling him back to her, but he resisted. With his shirt discarded, he started working on the buttons of hers. He took care, not only because he didn't want to tear her buttons but because he suddenly felt the need to slow down and enjoy this time with her. He'd never been one to tear the wrapping paper from his presents. He'd been the type to work the tape free and ease the paper from the box so he could build the anticipation.

Releasing the last button of her shirt was even better than all the birthday and Christmas presents combined. Her breathing was shaky and shallow by the time he slid his fingers into the opening he'd created. Easing one side open, he slowly released his breath as her lacy nude bra was exposed. He delicately scooped the globe of her breast into his palm and squeezed tentatively, brushing his thumb over the point of her nipple.

"Are you trying to kill me?" she whispered. "For God's sake, Phil." Pressing her hand to his, she tightened his hold on her breast as she arched into him. "I'm not going to break."

He laughed quietly. "I'm just admiring you."

"That's very sweet," she stated. "Maybe you could do that after."

Meeting her gaze, he grinned. "Are you in a hurry?"

"We have"—she pulled his hand from her breast to check his watch—"about an hour and ten minutes before you have to leave me. Admire me when we have time to spare."

He tried to fight his smile. "That could be a while."

"I'll wait."

Resting his forehead to hers, he kissed her lightly. "It's important to me that you know that I care about you, and I—"

She kissed him firmly, cutting him off.

"And," he continued when she leaned back, "I respect you. And—"

Staring into his eyes, she seemed to be scrutinizing him. Then she planted her palms against his chest and pushed until he sat back. When she was untangled from his body, she stood. For a moment, he thought she was going to tell him she'd changed her mind, but she grabbed his hand and led him through her house right to her bedroom.

When she faced him, she had her usual sarcastic tilt to her lips, but her eyes were on fire. She pulled her shirt off, letting it fall to the floor, and then reached behind her back and released the zipper on her skirt. The material pooled around her feet, leaving her standing in her underwear and a pair of white, open-toed heels. She kicked her skirt away, standing with her hands on her slender hips as he soaked in every inch of her.

His gaze landed on a tattoo just above her panty line. A bright red cherry seemed to have a secret meaning, but he knew it didn't mean what it implied. Every passing moment proved there was little innocence left in this woman. She was bold and confident and experienced. When she took a deep breath, the gem that decorated the piercing in her belly button caught his attention.

He lightly traced the ink with his fingertip, listening to her breath catch. The surge of nervousness that had made him feel uncertain just a few minutes before dissipated. "Do you have any other tattoos?" he whispered.

She grinned. "One. Find it."

Lowering his gaze, he skimmed it over her pale legs, her thin ankles, and then her arms, not finding a sign of another tattoo. He moved behind her, letting his hand linger on her stomach. He grinned at the Wonder Woman logo outlined on her shoulder blade. He pressed his lips against it before moving his kiss up her neck. "You're beautiful," he whispered when his lips found her ear. "Thank you for letting me admire you."

He lightly traced the spot where her bra hooked in the middle of her back. "May I release this?"

"Please do."

It'd been some time since he'd released that type of eye-and-hook closure, especially one-handed, but he managed to unsnap her bra. He eased the straps down her shoulders and over her arms. Standing behind her, he cupped her breasts and pulled her against him. Her head fell back to his shoulder. Squeezing, pinching her nipples as he did, he took a long, slow breath before lowering his hands. Sliding his fingers under the waistband of her underwear, he eased them over her hips.

Lowering to his knees behind her, he teasingly moved the material down her legs and then over one foot at a time. When she was standing there in nothing but her shoes, he gripped her hips and turned her. She was perfect. Everything about her. Leaning forward, he lightly kissed the cherry before leaning his head back to look at her.

She growled softly. "Okay. You've had long enough. We're going to run out of time." Grabbing his hand, she pulled him up and started working on releasing his belt as he toed off his shoes.

When they were both naked, she pulled him to her bed, opened her nightstand, and pulled out a condom.

"Ribbed for her pleasure," he commented after looking at the packet she held out for him.

Smirking, she said, "The only reason it doesn't vibrate, spin, and automatically find my G-spot is because nobody has invented that yet."

He chuckled. "I'll buy a carton when they do."

"Oh, I'll have them on preorder." She tugged the blankets back as he ripped the condom open and secured the protection in place.

By the time she lay back, parting her legs to accept him, he had to agree. He'd wasted enough time. No, not wasted. That wasn't the right word... Time cherishing her could never be wasted. But he was definitely ready to move on to what was going to happen next.

Slithering up her body and settling between her thighs, he met her gaze. Placing a light kiss on her lips, he teased her with his tongue before leaning back. She gasped and he groaned as their bodies joined. As if he didn't already know, that was the moment that convinced him Mallory O'Connell had been heaven-sent just for him.

CHAPTER NINE

*M*allory shivered and hunkered down deeper in the fleece-lined blanket wrapped around her. Watching a movie outside had seemed like a great idea when she'd set up the makeshift projector. Jessica had been wowed as soon as the image appeared on the side of the house. She still was. She'd finally stopped eating popcorn, but her gaze was fixed on the side of Phil's house, watching the superheroes save the day. She didn't seem to be cold at all, but another chill rolled down Mallory's spine. Summer was approaching, but not fast enough apparently.

"This was a terrible idea," Mallory whispered to Phil.

"No," he said just as quietly as he glanced at her. "This was an awesome idea."

"It's freezing out here."

"Want me to go grab you a sweatshirt?"

Actually, what she wanted was for him to come closer and

snuggle against her so she could steal his body heat...and maybe so she could feel his hands on her. Definitely so she could feel his hands on her. However, he jumped up and rushed inside before she could counter the sweatshirt offer.

After making love earlier in the week, they had agreed that they had to be careful not to get handsy in front of Jessica. Once they were certain they had a future together, they could let Jessica in on their relationship. Until then, as far as Jess was concerned, they were still just friends. She understood that was for the best and wholeheartedly agreed—she just hoped it wasn't too long before Phil was ready to tell his daughter he and Mallory were dating.

Being near him made it nearly impossible to keep her hands to herself.

Glancing at her watch, she checked the time. Jessica's bedtime was getting closer and closer, and Mallory's anticipation was growing. She and Phil usually called it an evening soon after Jess went to bed, but tonight Mallory planned to stick around. At least long enough to have a real good-night kiss with the guy.

Within minutes, Phil was handing her yet another layer to pile on her body. She tugged his bulky sweatshirt on as quickly as she could, letting as little body heat leave her as possible before wrapping the blanket around her again. She stopped moving when the scent from the sweatshirt wafted up to her.

Phil. The shirt smelled like Phil. Musky. Spicy. Manly. Damn, she wanted to get lost in his scent. She wanted to bury her face in his chest as he wrapped his arms around her and stay there until he made her leave.

She cast a quick glance his way. He was watching her, and when their eyes met, she suspected he was having the same longing she was. Ever since they'd popped the top on that particular need, that seemed to be all she could think about. She didn't think his desires were that much different. She couldn't stop herself from smiling.

Burrowing deeper in her blanket, Mallory tugged the neckline of his sweatshirt up over her nose and drew a deep breath. The scent was like a tonic that soothed whatever might have been ailing her.

A strange sense of peace and belonging surrounded her. She could see herself here, sitting in his backyard, watching movies by the little bonfire while Phil popped the corn over the flames and Jessica begged for just one more toasted marshmallow. This was a life she could see herself in. A place where she fit. A place where she wanted to be.

She was contemplating what that meant when she was gently nudged.

"Movie's over," Phil said.

She turned her attention to the wall, where the credits were rolling. How the hell long had she been sitting there sniffing Phil's shirt and fantasizing about movie night in the backyard?

"Thank goodness," she said by way of distraction. "I can't feel my toes."

"That was awesome." Jessica threw her arms up like she was on a roller coaster. "We have *got* to do this again!"

Phil kept his gaze on Mallory. "Maybe we should wait for warmer weather, Punk. Mal looks like an ice cube over there."

Mallory laughed. "I feel like an ice cube."

"Don't forget your blanket," Phil called when Jessica darted toward the house. She came back, gathered her belongings, and then called for Lucky to follow her. The dog was learning to manage with the cast and was able to hop up and waddle along. He'd turned into Jessica's shadow but seemed to have figured out that he should wait to follow until Phil was done reminding her to pick up that, or don't forget this, or take the dog with her.

With regret, Mallory unburied herself and went to work on dismantling the projector.

Phil started snatching up blankets. "That was really fun, Mal. Thanks for suggesting it."

"I thought you guys would enjoy this. But let's wait for summer before doing it again."

She followed him into the house and put her laptop in her bag while he dropped the blankets on the sofa. She had the sudden urge to suggest that he spread them on the floor instead. Maybe build a fire. Cuddle a little to get her warm. That kind of sappy stuff had never appealed to her before, but for some reason she could actually picture the romantic scene unfolding with Phil. He was a nice guy, a sensitive and considerate guy. He'd proven by the way he insisted on admiring her body before having sex with her that he likely wouldn't need hints dropped about preparing a nice, seductive evening. He seemed ready and willing to play into a woman's need to be seduced.

"I'm going to get Jess in bed," he said. "Wanna hang out for a while?"

Excitement shot through her. "Yeah. Sounds good."

He disappeared down the hallway, and she took a long, slow breath, looking at the pile of blankets. Jessica's excited voice bounced through the house, and Mallory had a sudden realization. That kid was wound up on a serious sugar buzz and movie high. She wasn't going to sleep anytime soon. If Mallory's past experiences of a sugar-buzzed Jessica were any indication, she'd be up to use the restroom, to get water, and to ask questions that simply couldn't wait until morning. And knowing Phil, he wasn't going to be firm enough to make her stay.

There would be no blanket in front of a crackling fire tonight. Or probably any night that Jessica wasn't having a sleepover with her grandparents. They were definitely going to have to make more requests of their friends and family to take Jessica for the night.

"Huh," Mal grunted with a sudden realization as to why she'd spent at least two nights a month with one of her uncles. Her mother had told her it was good for her to bond with her cousins, but Mallory finally understood her single mom was probably having her own kind of sleepovers. *Ick.* "How did I not figure that out sooner?" she asked herself.

"Hey," Phil called. "Jess wants you to come say good night."

Mallory put her hand to her chest as she widened her eyes as if to humbly ask, *Me?* She wasn't sure why she was surprised; she and Jessica had gotten pretty close, but bedtime seemed like a sacred father-and-daughter ritual that she had never even considered taking part in. Her heart seemed to have grown wings and taken flight, causing a painfully big smile to curve her lips. She had to be mindful of her pace so she didn't run into the kid's bedroom.

Reminding herself to be cool, chill out, and definitely control the urge to squeal, she walked into Jessica's bedroom. Her heart lifted again when she saw the poster-sized collage of photos from the comic book convention that Mallory had put together and had printed for Jessica. She didn't know why she was so happy to see it hanging on the wall. She supposed part of her expected the girl to toss it aside and never look at it again, but the carefully put-together poster was hanging on the wall right beside her bed, and Mallory felt a surge of pride.

That surge melted into a big, gushy warm center that filled her chest when Jessica stopped fluffing pillows and smiled up at her.

"Ready for bed?" Mallory asked.

Jessica opened her arms, silently asking for a hug. Mallory sat on the edge of the bed and squeezed her tight before putting a kiss on her head.

"Get tucked in." Mallory held the blanket up so Jessica could scoot down and rest her head on the rosy-pink pillowcase.

"Can we draw tomorrow? I want to learn to make comic books."

"Yeah. Let's draw tomorrow."

"I love you, Mallory," Jessica whispered.

Mallory gasped and then smiled that giant, face-cracking smile that she kept getting these days. "I love you, Jess. Sleep well, okay?"

"Okay."

Pulling herself from Jessica's bedside was probably the hardest thing Mallory had had to do since she'd moved away from Stonehill. She had that same sense of separation anxiety. Silly as it seemed, she just wanted to sit there and watch Jessica drift off to sleep. Brushing her hand over the little one's dark hair, she managed to get to her feet and head for the door. She stopped in her tracks, however, when she caught Phil standing in the doorway. Something in his eyes didn't seem to be as serene as the feeling in Mallory's soul. He seemed...upset. The somberness in his eyes gave her pause.

Had she done something wrong?

The look in his eyes faded as he threw a forced smile her way and stepped back to let her out of the bedroom. Slipping by him, she headed to the living room while he said one last good-night to his daughter.

The words that passed between Jessica and Mallory shook Phil to the core. He hadn't expected to hear that coming from Jessica or for Mallory to respond in kind. Fear took hold of his gut. This was exactly what he'd been trying to avoid all these years. The bond Jessica had formed with Mallory had become too strong too quickly. His daughter had a heart so big and so open that anyone could just walk right in and she'd happily accept them. While that was a wonderful trait, Phil's job was to make sure anyone who walked in wasn't going to turn around and walk out again.

Hearing Jessica whisper that she loved Mal was sweet on the surface but made his stomach turn in on itself. Mallory was great. She was sweet and considerate. But at the end of the day, what did they really know about her? He had no idea what she wanted for her future, other than to draw. What kind of financial stability could there possibly be for comic book artists? Or real estate agents? Selling houses was her day job. That didn't seem very stable either. The fact that Annie had made a career of the industry didn't comfort his concern.

What would happen if she finally accepted that living in California didn't mean she'd abandoned her mother? She could change her mind about being in Stonehill. She could want to move back to the West Coast. Phil planned to never leave. He finally had the stable life and family connections he'd been wanting all his life. He wasn't going to leave that behind. And he definitely wasn't going to uproot his daughter again.

Having Mallory in his life was fun. She brought out the lighter side of him and Jessica, but she also brought so many unknown variables. They weren't in a relationship. He had no right to try to pin her down on answers to these questions, but it wasn't fair of her to insert herself into Jessica's heart if she didn't plan to stay there for the long run.

This was exactly why he'd avoided dating.

Damn it.

He never should have let his parents plant seeds in his head about needing a woman in his life to fill a void they felt Jessica had. He never should have let Mallory in this fast.

A darkness started low in his gut, working its way up his chest and blocking out the light that she'd brought into his life the last few weeks. He had to take a step back, slow this train down before it jumped the tracks. He had to think twenty steps ahead so he knew what to anticipate to make things the best that he could for Jess.

He'd lost sight of that objective where Mallory was concerned. Being with her allowed him to stop looking so far into the future and focus on the now, but focusing on today without concern for tomorrow was a recipe for disaster. He'd learned that not just from bouncing around place to place growing up but by marrying a woman who could so easily walk away from her life. He had to be the one to build and maintain the foundations for himself and his child. He couldn't expect anyone else to do that, and part of that process was keeping an eye on the future to make sure the path was as smooth as possible.

Mallory had a way of distracting him, and distractions left room for missteps that he couldn't afford, not where Jessica's happiness was concerned.

That was so much easier said than done, he realized as he entered the living room to find Mallory explaining the importance of cleaning up after himself to Lucky. Something about a clean home equating a clean mind. He found that amusing considering how many trinkets she had scattered about her living room and office. But Lucky was enthralled, wagging his tail as he listened while she folded the pile of blankets Phil had dropped on the sofa.

Phil didn't blame the dog for looking like a spell had been cast over him. Mallory's voice was smooth and sweet like honey and her movements so fluid she made folding a blanket look sexy as hell. Spikes of short blond hair had escaped from her ponytail, making her hair look unkempt, and Phil thought he'd never seen someone dressed as tempting as Mallory O'Connell while swimming in the sweatshirt she'd added to her many layers. Well, other than Mallory O'Connell when she was standing in her bedroom in nothing but her underwear and a pair of heels.

As she dropped the last neatly folded blanket on the pile, she put her hands on her hips and eyed the dog. "Don't even think about climbing up there, do you hear me? I know what you're thinking. Your place is on the floor."

Lucky whimpered, wagged his tail, and panted until she leaned down and scratched his ears.

"That's one lucky dog," Phil said, finally making his presence known.

"Hence the name," she retorted, as had become the running joke the last few days.

She smiled at him, and he fell under the same spell as Lucky. Phil didn't even realize he was closing in on her until he was so close he had to tilt his face down to look into her eyes. Bringing his hands to her cheeks, he brushed his thumbs over her soft skin as her breath quickened. Her lips parted, and he had to smile because she reminded him of a woodland fairy for some reason. Maybe she was, because there was definitely something magical and hypnotic about her, something so carefree and alive that didn't seem natural. Something that made all his fears and reservations and plans fade away.

Staring into her starry eyes made him feel lost in a strange and comforting way, as if he'd fallen into a dream. He could let go of his stress when she was near. That was something Phil had never been able to do. In his mind, he knew he should be drawing the lines right now, laying down the rules, and setting the expectations. He needed to explain the boundaries and why they were necessary, but he couldn't. Boundaries didn't make sense when he was looking at this woman.

Instead of pushing her back a step, he pulled her closer, wrapped his arms around her, and secured her against him. Like a base jumper standing on the edge of a cliff looking down into a beautiful abyss, Phil held his breath to work up the courage to take the leap.

Just jump. Just do it. For once, just be brave.

Tilting her head back, he kissed her the way he hadn't been able to since leaving her house after ravaging her body. His kiss was a slow enticement to make her forget everything else, the way she made him forget his need to protect himself and his daughter from her powers.

He brushed his tongue along her lip. She opened her mouth in response, and he delved in. A fire ignited between them, consuming him, as it had the last time they were alone together. His tightly woven control burned to ashes as her body melted into his. Tugging at the shirt she was buried inside, he slid his hand under the hem, only to find another shirt. He managed to get underneath that and found another layer.

"How many shirts are you wearing?" he panted after tearing his mouth from hers.

She giggled. "Four."

He pulled at one more round of material before finally finding the warmth and softness of her skin. He sighed as he pressed his fingers into her lower back. "That's better," he whispered, resting his forehead to hers.

She yanked at his shirt, too, only he hissed when she rested her palm against his skin. She turned her fingers in, making sure every inch of ice-cold flesh touched him.

"Your hands are freezing," he gently chastised.

"Warm them up." The deep and sultry tone she'd used was something he'd only ever heard once before from her—in her bed. Her voice was always smooth, always soothing. This was something else. This was the most seductive music he'd ever heard. A true siren song. Those three little words struck a chord he couldn't remember anyone ever strumming before. The vibrations rolled through him, settling low in his stomach and catching the ember that had been burning.

Cupping the back of her head, he held her, forgetting about the icicles she had pressed against his spine, as he gave her another scorching kiss. He could kiss her forever. Her lips felt soft against his. Instead of strawberries, this time her mouth was sweet like the s'mores they'd made with a hint of salt from the popcorn he'd popped over the fire. Just like everything about her, the taste she left on his tongue had so many layers he couldn't possibly make sense of them all; he simply knew they worked in conjunction to make something so perfect he had a hard time trusting it.

Lucky whimpered and pawed at Phil's leg.

He pulled back and they both looked down, startled to find they had an audience. The dog whimpered again. He used that particular noise to tell his humans that he needed to go outside.

"Couldn't wait, huh?" Phil muttered. Focusing on Mallory, he sighed. "Don't move."

"Wouldn't dream of it."

Opening the back door, he ushered the pup outside and stood peering out at the dark. Actually, he was watching Mallory's reflection in the glass, smiling as she brushed her hands over her hair and dragged her palms over her thighs. She seemed nervous. But then another reflection caught his attention. Jessica.

"Mallory," she said. "I need water."

Phil turned to tell her that she didn't. She had a cup of water beside her bed, but Mallory held her hand out and Jessica rushed to meet her. Hand in hand they walked toward the kitchen. That should have warmed his heart even more than Mallory's kiss had, but the image was more like ice water dousing the fire she'd ignited in him. Reality hit him again.

Someone was going to get hurt. And the odds were, that someone was going to be Jessica.

They returned just as Lucky came to the door. Phil let the dog in as Mallory coaxed her down the hall. A darkness shot through his heart. Suddenly he didn't want Mallory putting Jessica to bed. He didn't want Jessica to start to think that was Mallory's place. Mallory's role was a friend, their buddy. She was silly and fun and had no place tucking Jessica in.

Rushing down the hallway, he inserted himself into the back-to-bed routine as casually as he could. "Okay, Punk," he said. "Mallory doesn't want to put you to bed every time you get up."

Mallory turned, as if to protest, but seemed to pick up on his reservations. A bit of the light seemed to dim in her eyes as she put her hand to Jessica's head. "See you tomorrow, kid," she stated, leaving him to tuck Jessica in, as was his responsibility.

"Don't get up again," he warned Jess, though they both knew she wouldn't heed his warning. She never did.

"Night, Daddy," she whispered.

He turned off her light and closed the door, trying to squash whatever monster had risen from the darkness. He couldn't. He was unsettled by the expression of love between Jessica and Mallory. He wasn't ready for them to be that connected.

Rejoining Mallory in the living room, he cleared his throat. "She, uh, she's probably never going to go to sleep until she hears you leave."

Mallory's smile fell, as if she'd been slapped, but she quickly forced it back to her face. "Right. Yeah. I know how she is."

If he'd hurt her feelings, which he suspected he had, she covered well. She stepped to him, right against him, and tipped her head back. He wanted to dig his hands into her hair and hold her there as he devoured her. Instead, he offered her a quick, lackluster kiss.

"Night, Mal," he whispered, ignoring the confusion in her eyes.

CHAPTER TEN

Mallory hated when her mind wandered all on its own, leaving reality behind, but that very thing kept happening as she and Jessica sat with sketchbooks open and pencils scattered across Phil's kitchen table.

The night before had been amazing. Right up until Lucky needed to take a potty break and Jessica needed water. Phil always had a tendency to run warm to cool, but last night he went from Krakatoa to Antarctica in the span of a few minutes. His kiss had burned her alive, but by the time he returned from tucking Jessica back into bed, he had ice in his veins.

She had given up the idea of a night of romance, but for him to basically turn her out after kissing her like she was the only woman he'd ever wanted was a kick to the gut. And to her ego. He'd ushered her out with barely more than a friendly smile and shut the door behind her the moment she stepped onto his porch.

She was nervous to see him today. Before their uncomfortable goodbye last night, Phil had asked if Mallory could leave work early and pick Jessica up from school while he went with his parents to meet with their adoption attorney.

Mallory had stood exactly where Phil had told her to. She smiled big when Jessica spotted her and came running. All her worries about Phil and his awkward behavior the night before disappeared as Jessica wrapped her arms around her waist and hugged her tight.

They'd gone through a drive-through to get a big box of chicken nuggets to share, all while Jessica chattered about her day and how cool Mallory's car was and could she please pick the music. Then, between handfuls of fries, she asked if Mallory had remembered her art supplies, because she'd promised to teach Jessica how to draw comics.

Mallory had been walking on air when they got to Phil's house. Lucky welcomed them with a wagging tail, clearly torn between greeting them and begging to go outside. He ran around the backyard, marking everything he could, while Jess and Mal ate their snacks. Once they were done, Jessica called him in while Mallory cleared the table and set out sketchbooks and pencils, ready to turn little Jess into her protégé.

However, the longer she'd sat in that space, looking at the very spot where Phil had turned on and off so damn quickly, the more a sense of dread settled in her tummy, squeezing the nuggets, fries, and ketchup into an uneasy mass.

Snapping back to reality when movement caught her eye,

Mallory smiled as Jessica held up a bright-red pencil and closed one eye as she stared at her drawing, as if assessing the alignment. "What are you doing?"

"I don't know, but Grandma does this when she's painting sometimes, so it must be important."

Chuckling, Mallory added the last bit of color to her drawing and turned her sketchbook around to show Jessica. "What do you think?"

Jessica's eyes widened as she drew a deep breath. "Is that me?"

Mallory looked at her drawing—a woman dressed all in pink with long brown hair and broad facial features. "Well. She's *inspired* by you."

"I've never seen a superhero with Down syndrome before."

"Then it's about time, don't you think?"

Jessica beamed proudly. "What's her name?"

Dropping her sketchbook back on the table, Mallory shrugged. "You're so great at coming up with names. What do you think we should call her?"

She thought only for a moment. "Let's call her Super Punk."

Smiling at the nickname Phil used for his daughter, Mallory agreed. "Perfect." She wrote the name in a graffiti-style text at the bottom. "How's that?"

"I like it."

Tearing the page free, Mallory held it out. "For you."

Jessica lifted the page, thoughtfully examining the drawing. "What are her powers?"

Mallory should have known to have an entire backstory

sorted out before showing the image. Jessica was inquisitive like that. She always wanted to know the why and the how so she could soak up as much information as possible. She reminded Mallory of how she used to be as a kid. Glancing at Lucky, Mallory said, "Rescuing dogs. She goes around the city at the speed of light, rescuing stray dogs and finding them forever homes."

Lowering the picture, Jessica met her gaze. "All animals. She'd rescue *all* animals."

That crazy sense of warmth spread through Mallory's chest. Of course Jessica would want to save all the animals. Her heart was too big to just save one kind. "Yes, she would."

"Can she have a sidekick that looks like Lucky?"

"Naturally." Taking the paper back from Jessica, Mallory started erasing a section of background color as she examined the black mixed breed sleeping at their feet. She selected a black pencil and swiftly added the pup. When she gave the picture back to Jess, Super Punk had a furry sidekick with a fancy chest shield that boasted the letter L on it.

Jessica laughed as she slid to the floor and showed it to the dog. "Look at us, Lucky. We're comic book heroes." After Lucky sniffed the drawing and licked Jessica's cheek, she jumped up and hugged Mallory. "I love it."

"I'm glad."

Leaning back, she looked into Mallory's eyes. "I'm glad you're here."

"Me, too."

Her smile widened as she looked over Mal's shoulder. "Daddy, look! Look what Mal drew for me."

Phil examined the picture of Super Punk and Lucky. He faked a smile for Jessica's sake, but Mallory could see through him. He didn't seem pleased. In fact, he seemed a little offended. She wondered what she'd done wrong in the picture. Maybe making a disabled superhero wasn't something he approved of; maybe he was worried Jessica might get some kind of idea about having powers. Or something equally as odd. Because nothing else seemed to make sense as she tried to understand his hesitancy to meet her eyes.

However, when she considered where he'd been—with his parents and their attorney, going over what needed to be done for Mira's adoption—she suddenly feared something hadn't gone as planned. She'd been hoping for Kara and Harry's sake that the adoption would go smoothly, but the anxiety in Phil's eyes implied otherwise. Maybe Lynn had changed her mind about giving up her parental rights. That would be terrible, considering her lack of interest in Mira's health and safety.

If she decided to keep Mira, that would put so much strain on Harry and Kara and in turn on Phil. He liked to act as if his mom's determination to help Mira was just some whim that she was having, but Mallory knew he worried for Mira, too. And not just because the baby was a handful for his parents. He might have chosen a different route of protecting the baby, but he was just as concerned for her as his parents.

He tried to hide that part of him that he worried was too

much like his mother, but her bleeding-heart ways were too ingrained in him. Mallory wished he could see they were far more endearing than he realized. The stress in his eyes made her heart ache. Something had gone wrong with the adoption proceedings. She was certain of that.

"That's great, Mal. Nice job." Phil handed the page back to Jess. "You should go put it on your wall with your other drawings."

"Can I?" she asked Mallory.

"Of course." She pushed herself up as Jessica ran out. Putting her hand on Phil's arm, she noticed how his muscle tensed under her light touch. "What happened?"

He creased his brow. "Nothing. Why?"

"You looked upset when you came in."

An obviously forced smile curved his lips. She had become familiar with his genuine smiles and the way they made light shine from his eyes. There was no light in his eyes at the moment, only sadness. "I didn't mean to," he said. "I'm just tired. It's been a long day."

That didn't ease her anxiety. "How did things go with the attorney?"

"Fine. He asked questions about my parents' marriage and things like that. Just made sure they could provide Mira with a good home. Nothing major."

"Does he anticipate any issues?"

Phil shook his head and stepped around Mallory. "As long as Lynn signs the papers, everything should be fine. He suggested that they have an open adoption since they are already planning on telling Mira about her birth mother. He said that could help smooth over any reservations Lynn may have." He picked up the drawing Jessica was working on. "This is...um..."

He turned the notebook to Mallory.

Mal thought the drawing was pretty good for an eleven-year-old. Though the proportions were off and her lines were shaky, the picture was clearly meant to be the three of them—Phil, Jessica, and Mallory—holding hands while Lucky sat next to them.

"She's a pretty good artist," Mallory said.

"Mom has been teaching her from the time she could hold a pencil. She wanted to help Jess work on her fine motor skills. Since Jess liked to draw and paint, it kept her interested and gave her motivation to keep trying." As he looked at the picture again, the sadness in his eyes grew.

Mallory had that sense of dread again. "What's wrong, Phil?"

He dropped the book onto the table. "I didn't eat lunch. Want to order pizza?"

"Sure," she said as he moved away from her again.

He didn't have to ask what she wanted. They'd ordered enough pizza over the three months that she'd been back for him to know she liked everything but onions. Instead of listening to him call in the order, she walked down the hall to Jessica's room. She'd added Mallory's drawing to several others on the corkboard that covered the bottom part of one wall. She was standing back admiring the placement when Mallory gingerly knocked on the door.

Jessica gestured for her to come in. "I made it look like a gallery."

"I see that."

"Grandma had a gallery showing once. She didn't like it. She said it meant she'd confirmed."

Mallory chuckled. "Con*form*ed."

"Yeah. That. Anyway. I think she's a little bit crazy because when I grow up, I can't wait to have a gallery showing."

Mal sat on her bed. "You're going to be an artist when you grow up?"

"Just like you and Grandma. I don't want to be a confirmist like Dad and Grandpa."

"Con*form*ist. And I don't think your dad and grandpa conformed. They just enjoy what they do."

Jessica turned from her wall. "Are you a con*form*ist? Since you work for your mom now?"

The shadow that had formed over Mallory grew a bit denser. She hadn't considered that, but in a way she had conformed. "I guess. I could find a job doing graphic design again, but I want to help Mom's business. It's important to her, so that makes it important to me."

Sitting on the bed next to Mallory, Jessica seemed to ponder her answer. "Do you think Annie wants you to conform? Because I know Annie, and I don't think she'd want you to do that."

Mallory smiled a bit. "It's not that simple, Jess."

"Why?"

"Because Marcus needs help with the real estate agency. He took on a big responsibility when Mom got hurt and couldn't help as much anymore. I know the family business, too. I can help. It shouldn't all be on Marcus when I can help."

"So you are giving up what you want to do to help someone else?"

"I'm not really giving up what I want to do." She gestured toward the drawing on the wall. "That's what I really want to be doing. I wasn't doing that in California, either."

"Why?"

Yeah. Why? "I don't know. I guess I was scared people wouldn't like my work."

"I like your work," Jessica said with all the conviction she seemed to be able to muster.

Mallory ran her hand down Jessica's back. "Thanks, Jess. I think that's probably the best compliment I could ask for." She meant that, too. Sure, she'd love to get paid to draw comic books, but the reality of that was out of her reach right now. What wasn't out of her reach was making this kid happy, and she'd done that with her drawing. That was enough for now. The rest... Well, that would happen someday if she wanted it to. She'd find a way to balance O'Connell Realty, helping her mom, and drawing comics. Everything would fall into place. Someday.

Jessica blinked and grew serious. "You can call me Punk now."

A lump filled Mallory's throat. She might as well have been handed everything she'd ever wanted, because that was the feeling that swallowed her. She hadn't even realized she'd been waiting for permission to use Jessica's nickname until she'd been given it like the key to some majestic city. "Thanks, Punk," she whispered, because she couldn't seem to speak louder than that through her emotions.

"You're welcome, Mal," Jessica said casually, as if she had no idea how much she'd just touched Mallory's heart.

The sound of a clearing throat made them both turn toward the door. Phil looked about as distressed as he had when he'd first appeared in his living room. "Pizza's on the way. How about you pick out a movie to watch, Punk?"

"*Yes*," she hissed, jumping off the bed.

Mallory's sense of dread grew. Phil was clearly dismissing Jessica from the room. He didn't let her pick the movie they'd watch very often. He wasn't nearly as keen on ponies and unicorns as his daughter. Even though her tastes were turning more toward Marvel and DC Comics, he was hesitant to let her have the final say in their evening entertainment. The only reason he did now, it seemed, was to get her out of the room.

Standing, Mallory wiped her hands on her denim-clad thighs, feeling uneasy at the stress on his face. "You know we're probably going to end up watching something with Barbie dolls spontaneously singing, right?"

"I don't know. Batman has started to become a staple around here."

"Good," she said with an enthusiasm she didn't really feel. "Glad to see her world is expanding."

"Trust me. It's definitely a step in the right direction."

She started around him, but he put his hand lightly to her arm and she stopped. She looked at him curiously, but her gut was still twisting with anxiety at his increasingly dark mood.

"Thank you, Mallory."

"For what?"

He gestured toward the just-added drawing on Jessica's wall. "The way you've connected with Jess is amazing. Not everyone is as receptive to her. So many people treat her like she's going to break. Or like her disability is contagious. You've always been so relaxed around her. She really needs that kind of acceptance. Having you around has had a great impact on her. She talks about you all the time."

Even though his words sounded more like a scientific observation than praise, she couldn't help but smile. There was nothing she wanted more, it seemed, than to be accepted by that quirky preteen she'd grown so fond of. "She's had a pretty good impact on me as well. I adore her, Phil. I really do."

"Good. I'm glad you feel that way. But..." He blew his breath out. "It's a bit..."

Stuttering. Incomplete sentences. This wasn't going to end well.

Mallory tried to keep the smile on her face. Maybe if she didn't accept whatever he was trying to say to her, he wouldn't say it. "What?"

"Disconcerting."

Disconcerting?

There it was. The tip of the iceberg of his unease.

"Care to expand on that?" she asked, though she was internally begging him not to. She didn't want to know, didn't want to hear what was coming next. Rejection. She could see it so clearly now. He was rejecting her. Probably had been for a long time and she was just too blind and dumb to see it.

"She's really starting to care for you, Mallory. More than she should this soon."

"I care for her, too."

"You're just getting settled into this new life."

"New life?" She scoffed. "I grew up here, Phil. Mom started teaching me real estate as soon as I could do basic math. Nothing here is new."

"You know what I mean," he said, and his words sounded... shameful, as if he hated what he was saying but was saying it anyway.

Her heart, which had been filled with so much happiness the last few weeks, seemed to mock her. This had all been too good to be real. She'd known this was coming. "I'm not going to disappear on her if that's what you're thinking," she said. "I'm not going anywhere. My family is here."

"I know. I believe you. It's just..."

"What?" she pressed. He didn't respond, so she demanded again, "What?"

The sadness in his eyes grew and the creases between his

eyes deepened. "I'm just concerned that she's starting to get the wrong idea about us."

That was like being stabbed in the heart. "*Us?*"

"*Us.* You and me and her. The three of us."

A knot formed in Mallory's chest. Had she gotten the wrong idea about them, too? Because the way he had been acting certainly seemed like an invitation for her to enter his life. They'd made love just a few days ago, and the night before he'd kissed her with more passion than she had ever felt before.

But then that splash of cold had ended their evening. She seemed to be getting an explanation as to why. She'd wondered about his mood swing all day. Now she was beginning to realize it wasn't his mood that had changed; it was his heart. She swallowed hard as tears formed a ball in her throat.

"I just think that maybe we should take a step back," he said.

"A step back? To what? We've barely taken a step forward."

He drew a breath. "I shouldn't have asked you to babysit while I went to the attorney. She has a babysitter."

Ouch. "Well, you said the babysitter doesn't like picking her up from school because it's a madhouse. I didn't mind. Besides, it wasn't babysitting as much as it was two friends hanging out drawing a bunch of pictures."

Her attempt to sway him from the notion that she somehow didn't deserve to be there backfired. His frown deepened.

"You drew superheroes," he said. "Jessica drew pictures of us as a family."

"Did she say it was us as a *family*? Because it looked like the three of us just hanging out as we always do."

He sighed. "I'm not trying to be a jerk here, Mallory."

"I didn't say you were."

"Your tone is getting a bit defensive."

She took a breath, hoping to lose the edge she hadn't realized she'd had. Her frustration was mounting quickly and had been since the night before. Ever since he started this back-and-forth, hot-to-cold route. "I don't get where this is coming from, Phil," she said honestly and more gently. "I'm not trying to make Jessica think we're a family."

"I know that. You haven't done anything wrong."

"Really?"

"Listen, you don't have to try, Mallory. She's had it in her mind from the start. I shouldn't have let things get this far."

"Get this far? You mean you shouldn't have"—she glanced down the hall before whispering—"fucked me and made me think we were a couple? That I was important to you? Isn't that what you said before crawling into my bed?"

"It's not about that." Phil raked his hand through his hair, again looking like he was dreading his words. But if he were, he'd stop staying them. Instead, he explained, "You're here almost every night, and if you're not here, we're at your house. It's given Jessica the wrong idea."

She opened her mouth to protest, but he continued.

"Today my parents said she was telling them all about how she wants us to buy a different house when we get married. One that has a bigger yard for Lucky and an art studio for you two to share."

That gave Mallory pause.

"She's making plans that she has no business making," Phil continued. "She's dreaming of things that are never going to happen. When she realizes that, it's going to crush her. I can't let her get her hopes up."

Never going to happen. Not *might* never happen. But never going to happen. Marriage hadn't crossed her mind, hadn't even been on the radar. However, for him to say that it would *never* happen was fairly definitive and cut at her heart like a serrated knife. If he felt that strongly about it, why the hell had he been in her bed?

Oh. Right.

Her mother's voice from years ago rang through her mind. *Men only want one thing, Mallory Jane.*

Shaking her head, dismissing the latest sting to her ego, Mallory said, "You need to talk to her. Explain to her that we're all still getting to know each other and we aren't there yet."

"I've done that. I've explained that we're just friends," he said, and his statement of friendship cut her again. The words had felt like a lie to her, but clearly they were his truth. He didn't seem to notice how they'd hurt her. He simply continued explaining why Mallory no longer fit. "She's getting too invested in this. In you."

Okay. That was the last button, the final straw, the nail in the coffin. He'd just burned her one too many times. She narrowed her eyes at him, her confusion consumed by the anger his implication raised. "What in the hell makes you think I'm not worth Jessica getting invested in?"

"That's not what I'm saying."

"That's exactly what you're saying. You wanted me to be someone she could turn to. Now you're saying she's too invested in me. I can't be someone she turns to if she doesn't trust me, Phil. If she doesn't *invest* in me and if I don't *invest* in her."

He seemed surprised, genuinely surprised, that she was angry. "I just need you to back off a little bit, Mallory. That's all."

"Why? What did I do? What brought this on?"

"You didn't do anything."

"Bullshit," she spat under her breath so Jess didn't hear. She wanted to scream and yell and maybe even punch him in the stomach for being such a jerk all of a sudden. "You were all over me last night, and then you couldn't get rid of me fast enough. Now you want me to back off? What the hell did I do?"

He raked his hand through his hair and exhaled loudly. "I just don't want her to get hurt."

Tears pricked at her eyes. She didn't know if she was upset by his words, the insinuation that she'd ever hurt Jessica, or because he was very clearly putting an end to whatever they'd started. "I'm not going to hurt her," she practically begged. "I care about her."

"I know that. I know you wouldn't intentionally hurt her, but she's starting to count on things that aren't going to happen. We're not going to get married and have a big house and all the things she told my parents she wants."

There was that conviction again, that certainty that friendship was all he ever wanted from her. "So tell her that. Tell her the truth. But don't tell me to back off when I haven't done anything but be here for her, like *you* asked me to."

"Just some time, Mal. Just some time and space. Please."

"Fine. Whatever you want, Phil." Throwing her hands up, she slid by him and headed for the living room. "Hey, Jess," she said as cheerfully as she could. "I totally forgot I have to have dinner with my mom tonight."

"No," Jessica said dramatically. "I picked out an Avengers' movie just for you."

"Sweet. Tell you what," she said, putting her hand on Jess's. "We'll watch it next time I'm over."

"Tomorrow?"

Mallory glanced at Phil, who had emerged from the hallway. "Probably not tomorrow. I've got things to do. But soon. Okay?"

A loud sigh was followed by Jessica dropping back on the sofa. "Fine."

"Hey," Mal whispered. When Jess looked at her, pouting ever so slightly, she smiled. "I love you, Punk."

"Love you, Mal. Tell Annie hi for me, okay?"

"I will."

Grabbing her coat and her purse, Mallory didn't bother saying goodbye to Phil. The stupid jerk didn't deserve the nicety.

sh

Phil sank back on the couch, certain that Jessica was finally asleep and Lucky had made his final potty-break request. This was definitely one of those days when being a single parent wore him down to the bone. He was exhausted from her constant chattering and questions and making plans for the following weekend. Did he think Mallory would want to go to the children's museum? Did he think Mallory would bring the projector over again? Did he think they could make tacos instead of ordering pizza because Mallory told her that she really liked tacos? Did he think they could take Lucky for a walk at the lake with Mallory?

Everything was about Mallory. And not just in Jessica's mind, either. He couldn't stop seeing the hurt in her eyes as he stood there telling her that she needed to back off. Even though everything in him was screaming at him to shut his big fat mouth, he continued until she finally heard him and walked away.

Looking at his phone, he felt an unrealistic amount of disappointment that she hadn't texted him. Of course she hadn't. He'd done everything he could to pull the rug out from under her.

She wasn't stupid. He'd taken her to bed, and yeah, he'd implied they were a couple with more than just his actions. He'd held her in her bed, kissed her and stroked her soft skin over and over, telling her how he couldn't remember ever feeling the way he felt about her. They hadn't been cheap words, but they certainly seemed to be now. Their attraction was on a level he'd never delved to. His feelings for her were strong and real, and he suspected hers were as well. But then he'd told her right to her face there wasn't more to it than friendship.

She'd flinched. She'd actually flinched when he told they'd never have a future together. He wanted to kick himself in the ass for that. Instead, he opened his phone and looked at her social media pages. She was more active than he'd ever been, so all the evidence of their recent adventures had played out on her pages. The comic book convention, trying new restaurants, Lucky's first night at home, teaching Jessica new drawing techniques. Her page was filled with their short life together.

Damn. No wonder Jessica saw them as a family. Phil hadn't really considered how much they acted like one. Mallory had slipped into their lives so seamlessly, he hadn't even noticed how much she'd been there.

No. That wasn't quite true. He was probably just as guilty as Jessica, obsessing about her from the time she left until the next time she showed up, smiling like the sun.

Dropping his phone, Phil traded the photos for the lukewarm beer he'd opened but had been too distracted to drink. He hadn't slept the night before. He'd replayed kissing Mallory over and over in his mind. He'd tossed and turned and debated how far things would have gone if Lucky and Jessica hadn't interrupted. He wondered if she'd have been willing to let things go all the way to the bedroom. He certainly had been.

And that was a mistake.

Everything about being with her was a mistake. Not because

it was wrong but because it was too right. Too easy. She had a way about her that drew him in like a sunflower was drawn to the sun. She warmed him from inside in a way that he somehow felt he needed to survive. That was dangerous. Counting on her was dangerous. For him and for Jess.

If the heartbreak in Mallory's eyes was any indication, this was too dangerous for her, too. They'd all gotten too wrapped up in each other too fast. This was for the better. Definitely for the better. He had to save them all from themselves.

"Daddy?" Jessica asked.

He closed his eyes, not sure if he was frustrated that she was up again or thankful that she'd pulled him from his thoughts. Probably a mixture of both. "Yeah, Punk?" he asked, setting his beer down.

"Can I ask you something?"

She appeared at his side, and he smiled up at her. "Sure."

"Did you and Mallory fight? Is that why she left instead of watched a movie with us?"

Crap. Blowing his breath out, he shrugged. "Not a fight, really."

"Are you sure? Because you've been cranky since she left."

"Have I?"

Jessica nodded.

Patting the seat beside him, he waited for her to sit before kissing her head and snuggling her against him. "Sometimes grown-ups just have to have serious talks that aren't much fun."

"What did you talk about?"

Phil sighed as a memory of the hurt and confusion in Mallory's eyes slashed through his mind. "Mallory and I are just friends, Punk. You know that, right?"

She didn't respond.

"Friends who have fun together. Like you and your friends. We like to be around each other. But that doesn't mean we're ever going to...you know...be a family or anything like that."

Jessica sat quietly.

"I like Mallory," Phil said. "She's really nice."

"Is this because I asked you if you *liked her* liked her?" She looked up at him, and there was so much sadness in her eyes that his heart ached. He'd unintentionally hurt Mallory earlier, and now he was hurting Jessica. He just wished they both could see that he was stopping this now so Jessica didn't get hurt much worse later.

"I guess in a way it is," he said. "I don't want you to think that we're ever going to be more than friends."

"But you could be. Mallory doesn't have a boyfriend. I asked."

He smiled. "I know she doesn't."

"So *you* could be her boyfriend."

He swallowed the knowledge that for a few short days, he kind of had been her boyfriend. He'd certainly blown that. "I don't want to be her boyfriend, Punk," he said, knowing that wasn't really the truth.

Her face melted as the hope in her eyes dimmed. "Why? What's wrong with her?"

"Nothing. There is absolutely nothing wrong with Mallory. I think she's great."

"So be her boyfriend. She'd say yes if you asked, Daddy."

"Jess—"

"I'll ask her for you," she offered, her eyes lighting up again. "I know she'll say yes."

"Jessica, I don't want to be anybody's boyfriend. Not right now."

Her little lip trembled. "Why?"

He hugged her close. "Because I have everything I want and need right here. I have you and Lucky. And I have Grandma and Grandpa."

"And Mallory."

He nodded slowly. "And Mallory. As my friend."

"But—"

"Jessica," he said more firmly, "I don't want a girlfriend right now. Okay? Grown-up relationships can be really messy. I don't want messy right now. Things are really great, right? We're doing great. We don't want to mess that up."

She wasn't getting it. She wasn't understanding. She was looking at him with the same confusion that Mallory had.

"I'm sorry," he whispered. "I know you want someone to be like a mom to you, and Mallory would be a good person for that."

"She loves me," Jessica whispered. "She told me so."

He nodded. "I know. And I believe her. I believe that she loves you very much."

"She would be my mom if you asked her to."

"It's too soon for that, Jess."

Her eyes welled. Tears—big, fat, broken-hearted tears—fell from her eyes. "Mallory loves me. She told me so. I don't care if you don't want her to be my mom, *I do*." She pushed herself up and stomped toward her bedroom.

"Jess?"

She didn't respond.

"Jessica!" He started to follow her but dropped back when her bedroom door slammed. He didn't have the strength to continue this conversation. Not tonight. He was running on fumes, and not just physically. He'd been emotionally tapped out since Mallory left. He couldn't keep analyzing this situation.

Carrying his beer to the kitchen, he dumped the near-full contents down the drain and tossed the bottle into the recycle bin. The photo of him, Mallory, and Jessica dressed in silly costumes mocked him from where it hung on the fridge by a Batman magnet—the one Mallory had bought as a reminder of the day—but he resisted the urge to look at it. He refused to be reminded yet again how much life she brought into this house, but those reminders were unavoidable. The hollow feel of the house reminded him that she was missing. As did the quiet as he readied for bed and the emptiness of his bed as he slid between the sheets.

Somehow, even though she'd never stepped foot inside his bedroom, he felt her absence there. Something inside him—

probably his mother—was telling him that his life didn't have to be like this. His home didn't have to feel so lonely.

But then he remembered how hurt Jessica looked at the idea of him and Mallory not being a couple. And that was before they even were a couple. He could only imagine how broken she'd be if he let them be a family, only to have that taken away from them sometime down the road.

No. It was better this way. Better to keep Mallory strictly in the friend zone so he and Jessica wouldn't be shattered when things ended.

Things always ended.

allory didn't lift her eyes from the now-cold cup of coffee nestled between her palms when Annie eased into a chair at the break room table next to her. Mallory had tried to avoid her mother all morning, but she knew that only made Annie more worried. The maternal concern in the office seemed to rise by the minute. Not just Annie's; her aunt Dianna had picked up on her melancholy mood, too. Even Marcus had asked her if she was doing okay.

She wasn't. She hadn't slept a wink the night before. She'd just kept rolling the last few months over and over in her mind, trying to figure out what she'd done wrong. Nothing, according to Phil, but that couldn't be true. If that were true, he wouldn't have kicked her to the curb.

Annie slid a chocolate-chip muffin into Mallory's line of vision. "Wanna talk about it?"

"Not really."

"Phil?"

Mallory pried her fingers from the cup and picked at the muffin, peeling off a chunk but then setting it aside. "You dated when I was growing up, didn't you?"

"Of course."

"But I never met anyone. At what point would you have introduced me to someone? I mean, how deep into a relationship would you have had to be to let him get to know me?"

Annie nodded. "Definitely Phil."

Dropping another chunk of muffin onto the table, she brushed her hands. "Do you think the only reason he let me get to know Jessica is because he isn't attracted to me?"

"Wait. Can we take a step back?"

Mallory grated her teeth together. "Everybody wants to take a goddamned step back."

Annie frowned. "I just mean, I'm not up-to-date on what's happening. Can you fill me in?"

Sinking back, she explained, "Everything was great. Or so I thought. Jessica is great, she's wonderful. Phil... I can't figure him out. One minute he acts like we're this perfect little unit; the next he acts like there's no room for me in his life."

"He's always been very protective of Jess."

"He's not being protective, Mom, he's using her as an excuse not to get close to me. Why would he do that? I mean, unless he just doesn't want me around. Maybe I'm just too stupid to catch the clues he's been dropping." She pressed her hand to her forehead, discounting that idea. If he didn't want her around, he wouldn't have made love to her. Would he?

Annie squeezed Mallory's hand. "I'm having a hard time keeping up here, sweetie. Can you tell me exactly what's going on?"

"I offered to be his void-*filler* for Jessica." Damn. Even she could hear the resentment in her voice. Closing her eyes, she took a breath and tried again. "Like you told me about a hundred times, Jessica needs someone, and I want to be that someone. I'm totally cool being that someone."

"But?"

"But...I really care about Phil, too. Probably more than I should. He's nice, Mom. Like the way Marcus is. Genuinely nice. He is such a good dad, and he worries about his parents, and he's just..."

"Perfect?"

She rolled her eyes. "Not even close. He's a big, stupid idiot."

"Men tend to be that way."

Mallory frowned deeply, creasing her brow with the confusion that kept overwhelming her. "Things were going great between us. We were getting closer, and then..."

"And then?"

She glanced up. Even if she was an adult, confessing to her mom that she was intimate with a man felt awkward, but Annie didn't look freaked out that her little girl might have taken some of those steps with someone. She looked worried. "We went on a date and he shut down. I mean, like, he flipped a switch. Hot to cold like that." She snapped her fingers to explain how quickly things had changed. "He told me we need to put some space between us because he's worried Jessica is too invested in me."

"He got scared," Annie clarified.

"Scared of what?"

"Honey, you have to remember this isn't just about you and Phil. This is about Jessica, too. It's his job to protect her."

"Not from me."

"I didn't mean from you. I mean from life. She feels things more deeply than most people."

Mallory shook her head, refusing to believe that she would ever be capable of hurting Jessica. "No, this is about Phil and his damned insecurities. He acts like he's the only one who ever had someone walk out on him." She didn't even know she was about to cry until tears filled and overflowed from her eyes before she could stop them. "He acts like I don't know how it feels to have a hole in my heart. My dad left, too."

Annie sighed. "Oh, Mal."

Wiping her face, she blew out her breath, trying to get control of herself. "I know we were better off, Mom, but even knowing that, it's always been in the back of my mind. I always felt like there was something wrong with me. That Dad—and I only call him that for dramatic effect—wasn't there because of me. Phil grew up feeling that way, too. And now Jessica is feeling that way. I don't want her to feel that way. It sucks."

"I'm sorry."

"It's not your fault."

"It is."

"No, it's not." Mallory covered Annie's hands with her own. "We *were* better off without him. Jessica is better off without her mother. But knowing that doesn't fix what's missing. For any of us. We're all broken, and we could help each other if he'd just stop being such a...*man*."

Annie stroked her hand over Mallory's head. "I pushed you into this. I pushed you into being a friend for Jessica. I shouldn't have—"

"No. You were right. Jess is great, and she does need someone. I'm going to be there for her. I just have to find the right balance so Phil doesn't freak out."

"Maybe he's right. Maybe you just need to give him some time and space to realize that he does want you to be part of that little unit you three had created."

"What about Jess? Is she supposed to sit on the sidelines until her dad pulls his head out of his ass?"

"I am very confident that you and Phil can figure out how to be around each other long enough to not leave Jessica on the sidelines. If Phil is worried that Jessica is getting the wrong idea about you and him, then it is up to you and him to remove that idea from her head. Without tossing her aside. You can still be there for Jessica and limit the amount of time the three of you are together."

Leaning forward, Mallory put her hands to her eyes, hoping to stop the next round of tears. "This is so unfair to her."

"Yes, it is. But that isn't your fault. You did what he asked, Mallory. You did what Jess needed."

Dramatically dropping her hands, she frowned at her mother. "I didn't want to be this person for her, you know? I thought that it was up to Phil to find someone who could be there for her, but he's never going to, Mom. You and Kara were right. He's never going to see that by keeping her in this safe little bubble, he's not protecting her. He's keeping her from making connections that she needs. I don't know how to make him see that."

"You can't." Frowning, Annie shrugged. "Mallory, I'll be honest. I had no idea you felt so hurt by your father leaving until you just told me. I should have known it. I should have seen it. But I didn't because I didn't want to."

"I didn't say that to upset you."

"I know that. But I chose to believe that having your uncles involved in your life was enough. Even after all the times you've commented about Marcus being your dad now, I didn't let it sink in."

Grinning, Mallory lightly tapped Annie's forehead, as she so often did to herself, and said, "You have brain damage. Remember?"

Annie chuckled and swatted playfully at her hand, but then she grabbed it and held it tight. "I didn't know, Mallory. And I guarantee you, Phil isn't seeing it in Jessica. I'm sorry. I wish I'd known. I don't know what I could have done, but I do wish I'd known."

"It's okay, Mom. We were okay. We're still okay."

"Better now that you have Marcus?"

Mallory nodded. "Yeah. Except when he gives me a hard time about my cooking."

"Well, sweetheart, you are a terrible cook."

Giggling, Mallory tugged at Annie's hand. "I got that from you."

Annie's smile faded. "If you want to find your father—"

"Marcus is my father." She nodded solidly. "Marcus is my dad. Best dad I could have asked for."

Blinking, Annie did a better job of stopping her tears from falling, but her eyes did get shiny from the sudden surge of dampness. "Be there for Jess as much as he will let you. She adores you."

"I know. I adore her, too."

Cupping Mallory's face, Annie smiled. "I love you, Mallory."

"I love you, Mom."

"But know this. I'll kill Phil if he makes you cry again. And I'll get away with it." She tapped her forehead and smirked.

Mallory laughed. But didn't completely dismiss the idea.

Stupid jerk.

Phil scowled at his computer screen. He'd been working on a graphic design proposal for three hours and his screen was still blank. Empty. Just like his fucking life. Shoving his mouse aside, he cursed under his breath, giving up any notion of having a productive day.

"That was dramatic," Harry said from Phil's office door.

"I'm not feeling this account. Maybe someone else should take it."

Walking into the small space allotted for Phil's creative thinking, Harry sat on the edge of the desk. "I have a feeling it's more than that. Want to talk about it?"

Phil shook his head. "Not really." Looking up, finally facing his father, he sighed. "Jesus, Dad. You look like hell."

"You don't look much better."

Frowning, he roughly ran his hand through his hair. "I... went on a date with Mallory."

Harry's brows show up. "Oh."

"And then I told her to give me space."

His brow creased. "Oh."

"She's done exactly what I asked. Not a single text or phone call since she stormed out on me yesterday."

Harry didn't seem to have much sympathy.

"Jessica's mad at me," Phil added. "She thinks Mallory should be my girlfriend, and when I told her I don't want a girlfriend, *she* stormed off."

Harry still didn't show any pity for Phil's situation.

"This is Mom's fault."

Finally, Harry responded. "I was waiting for that."

"What?"

"You think everything is your mom's fault, Phil. You always

have. You never want to take any responsibility for your own choices. Every time you screw up, you blame your mother or your childhood. You never want to step back and see that sometimes, it's you making bad decisions."

Phil's irritation doubled in a heartbeat. "What does that mean?"

"Your mom is worried about Jessica. She told you her concerns—which were valid, by the way—and suggested you find someone for Jessica to connect with. She didn't say a damn word about you getting romantically involved with her."

"She did. I specifically remember—"

"Her hoping you would but not forcing you to. Your mother didn't twist your arm until you went on a date with Mallory. Did she?"

Huffing, he shook his head. "No."

"She wants you to be happy. You *and* Jessica. And, if I might say, you've been happier the last few weeks than I've ever seen you. I'm guessing that had everything to do with Mallory O'Connell and not a damn thing to do with your mother."

Phil frowned. "Fine. I like Mallory, okay? I like her a lot."

"Why are you saying that like it's something to be ashamed of? Mallory is great. Jessica thinks the world of her."

"So does Mom."

"Is that such a turnoff, Phil? Having someone in your life that your mother likes is such a bad thing?"

He shook his head and sighed. "No. You're right. This has nothing to do with Mom. It's..."

"It's hard to trust someone after you've been burned."

Meeting his father's eyes again, Phil frowned. "That's not it."

"That is it."

"I have to be careful who Jessica gets attached to."

"Only if you think that person isn't worth her getting attached to, Phil."

The accusation stung, reminding him of what had seemed to hurt Mallory the most—the suggestion that he didn't think she was worth Jessica's affections. "What do you mean?"

Sliding from the desk, Harry pulled the extra chair in Phil's office close enough that when he sat, his elbows resting on his knees, there were just a few inches between the two of them. That close, Phil noticed that the gray in his father's dark hair had multiplied and the dark rings under his eyes had grown immensely in the last few weeks. The situation with Mira was taking a toll on him. Phil made a mental note to pop in and check on his parents. He'd been so caught up in his own conflicting issues, he'd forgotten his vow to help Kara and Harry out more.

"When I started dating my ex-wife," Harry said, "her boys were just a little bit younger than Jessica. They still had a lot of anger about their parents' divorce, and man, they didn't want me around. I did everything I could to break through to them, Phil. I took them to ball games, I bought them toys, I dropped in with pizza every Friday night, but nothing ever worked. They had so much resentment for me, I could practically breathe it in. Even with all that, the thing that really destroyed our marriage wasn't that her kids couldn't accept me but that she never bothered to try to convince them that I was worth accepting. I started to wonder if she felt the same way about me. That maybe I really wasn't good enough for them."

"This isn't the same."

"Maybe the situations aren't the same, but the underlying issue is. You don't think Mallory is good enough for Jessica."

Harry's words stabbed at Phil. "That's not true."

"It is."

"No. Mallory is great. Too great. *That's* the problem. She and Jessica accept each other *too* much."

"So you're jealous of their relationship?"

"No." Raking his fingers through his hair again, he blew out his breath. "There are no guarantees that Mallory is going to stick around, Dad. What if she decides to go back to California? What if she decided she doesn't want to settle down with me and Jess? What if…"

"What if your relationship ends and Jessica gets caught in the middle?"

"Yes," he stated firmly. "That's it. Right there. Jessica lost one mother. I don't want her to lose another one."

"Phil, no relationship comes with a guarantee. Mira lost one mother. Lynn can't hit the road fast enough."

"That's probably best for Mira."

"It is. But what if Kara hits the road, too? You know how she is. The moment she feels tied down, she gets the urge to run. Nothing says tied down quite like having a husband and kid."

Phil shook his head. "No. She wouldn't do that."

"How do you know? No one ever really knows what someone else will do. Kara could walk out at any time. *I* could walk out at any time. Nothing is guaranteed."

Creasing his forehead, Phil tried to understand what Harry was saying. "Are you guys having problems?"

His dad sighed and closed his eyes for a moment before looking at Phil like he'd totally missed the point. "No. Not today. Probably not tomorrow. But we will sometime, Phil. No relationship is smooth sailing forever. People change, people make mistakes, and people get hurt. Kids get hurt when their parents split. But that doesn't mean you should never have a relationship, that she should never know what it's like to have a maternal figure in her life. Mallory is good for her. Mallory makes her feel like she has something she has been missing her entire life. Yeah, Mallory could leave. Tomorrow, next week, or in ten years. She could walk away. But so could you. Actually, it sounds like you already did."

Phil shook his head. "I'm trying to do what is best for my daughter."

"I know that. Everyone knows that. You're doing a great job, Phil. You really are. But sometimes, trying too hard isn't the best thing. I know your mother regrets that she never let anyone close enough to you to fill that fatherly void for you. She thought she was protecting you, but now she sees that she was just scared of being hurt again. Whether you want to admit it or not, you are following right in her footsteps. You deserved better. So does

Jessica. If you can't let Mallory into your heart, that's your issue. But she's already in Jessica's. It isn't fair of you to put a wall around her because you want one around you."

Phil frowned. "She wants us to be a family."

"I know. She's told us. You had to see this coming, Phil. If not with Mallory, then Jessica would have wanted it with someone else. She's aching to have someone she can look to like a mom, Phil. *Aching*. In her soul. I understand if you can't give her that, but at least let her have Mallory as a friend."

"I didn't say they can't be friends," he stated, not caring that he sounded frustrated.

"So make that clear. With Jessica and Mallory. And then you stand by it, Phil. Because once you put those boundaries in place, you can't change them just because you want to. That's not fair to anyone."

He considered his father's advice before nodding. "I hear you. I do."

"Good. I'm heading out. We have another appointment with the attorney. Keep an eye on things here."

"Dad," he called when Harry stood. "Mom won't walk out. In case you're actually worried about that."

Harry smiled. "Maybe Mallory won't, either."

CHAPTER TWELVE

*P*hil wiped Jessica's tears. She'd been holed up in her room crying since he got home from work, and it was tearing him apart. Her babysitter said she'd been in her room since she got home from school. She thought something had happened, maybe someone had picked on Jessica, but Phil suspected the same thing was upsetting her that had put him on edge all damn day.

Mallory.

Finally, he'd ignored her insistence that he leave her alone and sat on her bed. "Come on, Punk. You gotta talk to me. What's going through your head?"

She sniffed as her bottom lip trembled. The movement was subtle, but it was enough to make Phil's heart crumble. He couldn't take seeing his little girl miserable. Seeing her cry was like having his soul ripped to shreds.

He ran his hand over her hair and gently patted her back. "Will you please sit up and look at me? Talk to me."

She sniffed and wiped her nose on the glittery purple sleeve of her My Little Pony shirt as she faced him. Phil opted not to remind her not to do that.

"I want Mallory," she said.

"Jess." Sighing heavily, he lifted her chin until she looked at him. "I know you do."

"Is she mad at me?"

"No." He swallowed. "Not you. Maybe a little bit at me."

"Why? What did you do?"

He sighed. "I told her I was worried you were getting too attached to her and that maybe she shouldn't come around for a while."

Her eyes widened. "Why would you tell her that?"

"Because it's true." He nodded toward her pictures. "Look at your drawings."

Jessica studied her gallery. All the pictures had a dark-haired man holding hands with a dark-haired girl who was holding the hand of a blond woman. Mallory. The woman was Mallory. Even in the pictures where Jessica tried to make her image look like Super Punk, there were pictures of Phil, Mallory, and Lucky in the background. Her drawings used to always be her dad and grandparents.

Jessica sniffed deeply, pulling Phil's attention from her gallery back to her tear-stained face. "I wished for her to come."

"What do you mean?"

"My birthday. Every year I wish for a mom. This year she came. She came, and everything was better." She narrowed her eyes and whispered accusingly, "You ruined it."

"No, honey. Listen."

"She was my friend."

"And she always will be," Phil said.

"You made her go away."

"Jessica—"

"Why can't you just let me have a mom? Everybody has a mom. Even Mira is getting Grandma as her mom. Everybody has a mom but me."

Phil lifted his hand to stop her rant. "Whoa. Who told you about Mira?"

"I'm not deaf, Daddy. I can hear you guys whispering. I know Grandma and Grandpa are adopting Mira. She's getting a new family, and it's not fair. I want a mom, too, but I don't have one because *you* let her leave."

He sat back, startled by her words. He'd never seen Jessica so angry at him before. Sure, she'd had temper tantrums and fits over the last eleven years, but he could actually feel her rage seeping into his pores.

"Jess," he said gently, "Mallory meant what she said—"

"I don't mean Mallory. I mean my *real* mom. Why didn't you make her stay? Why did you let her leave?"

Once again, her words caught him off guard. "I... Your mom was scared. We've talked about this before."

"You should have made her stay."

Phil swallowed hard as she started sobbing again. She turned from him and pressed her face in her pillow. He put his hand to her back, but she jerked away from him.

"Leave me alone, Daddy."

He patted her back one more time before getting up and leaving her to her tears. He didn't know what else to do.

sh

Mallory hesitated before knocking on Phil's door. She hadn't answered his call but had listened to his voice mail. He'd told her how upset Jessica had been all afternoon and begged her to stop by and talk to her. She hadn't given her actions a second thought as she jumped in her car and headed over. At least not until she was standing there, on the verge of facing him. Swallowing the lump in her throat, she rapped her knuckles against the door, causing Lucky to start barking on the other side.

Phil's voice was muffled, but he was clearly hushing the dog. He opened the door and seemed to have a hard time meeting Mallory's gaze.

She scoffed as she pushed by him. *Jerk*. "Jess in her room?"

"Has been all evening."

She shrugged out of her jacket and dropped it on the back of the couch as Lucky hobbled over to greet her. She scratched the dog's ears.

"Look, Mallory—"

Standing upright, she glared at him, sending emotional

daggers across the room. "Unless you plan on apologizing to me for being a gigantic ass, save it."

He shrank a bit before grinning. "I'm sorry I was a gigantic ass."

She didn't know what to say. She hadn't actually expected him to apologize.

"All this stuff with Mira's adoption and Lynn leaving is stirring up things I thought I'd resolved a long time ago. It certainly hasn't helped that Jessica has become obsessed with finding a mom. It's not an excuse for how I behaved. Just a reason."

She nodded. "I'm sure it isn't easy watching Lynn abandon her responsibilities."

"Mira's going to have a lot of insecurities growing up."

Mallory tilted her head. "We all do, Phil. Whether we have two parents or not. There's always something that makes us question our worth. Your mom took really good care of you and of Jessica, and she'll take good care of Mira. What Jessica is going through isn't a reflection of you or the way you raised her. She's just fixated on the thing that makes her different from her friends."

"She has Down syndrome, Mallory. There are dozens of things that make her different from her friends."

Mallory sighed. "Well, this is the thing that she has chosen to focus on. Maybe because it's the one thing that can be changed."

He gave a wry laugh. "Wow. I hadn't thought about it like that."

"Yeah. I know." She lowered her face as she took a deep breath. "Look, I'll still be here for Jessica. I care about her and want to be her friend. But you're right about us. We need some time and distance for a while."

He looked hurt. The prick actually looked hurt.

She didn't back down. "I think it's best for everyone if we keep our time around each other limited to me picking up Jessica or dropping her off. That should make it clear to her that you and I aren't more than friends. Okay?"

"Yeah," he said, so softly she almost didn't hear.

She headed down the hallway and gently knocked on Jessica's bedroom door. There was silence on the other side, so she turned the knob slowly and walked in. Her heart ached at the bundle on the bed. "Knock knock."

Jessica pushed the blankets down, and instead of the big smile Mal was used to, she was met with puffy red eyes and a trembling lip.

"Oh, baby." She sat on the bed and opened her arms. Jessica was hugging her a moment later.

"Don't listen to Daddy, Mal. Please. Please don't go away."

Hushing her, Mallory held her tight. She hadn't even realized how much Jessica had become a part of her life until Phil tried to shut her out. She had done her best not to think about the ache inside her, but sitting there holding her, Mallory thought maybe she could finally understand Phil's concerns. She would never do anything to hurt Jessica, ever, but if she and Phil got into a relationship and it didn't work out, Jess would be in the middle. There was no way to avoid that.

"Hey, Punk," she whispered. "Think you can sit up? I need to talk to you about something."

She lifted her head from Mallory's shoulder. "Did I do something wrong?"

"No. Not at all." Wiping Jessica's cheeks dry, she offered her a reassuring smile. "Your dad told me some things that you said to Grandma and Grandpa."

"What things?"

"That someday your dad and I might get married. That we might get a new house. Do you remember saying that stuff?"

She looked down and nodded.

Mallory tucked her hair behind her ear. "You're not in trouble, Jess. It's okay to talk about the things that you want. Everybody has things they want. But your dad and I... We're just friends. Friends don't get married."

"Your uncle Paul and Dianna were friends and they got married. I heard Grandma and Dianna talking about him for a long time. Dianna said they were just friends, but Grandma told her they were going to be a couple. And now they're married. And Annie and Marcus were friends. Now they're married, too."

Mallory nodded. "You're right. About Paul and Dianna and Mom and Marcus. But things are different between your dad and me. We really are just friends."

Her shoulders sagged and she crawled from Mallory's lap to

the pile of pillows. "I know Dad can be a stick in the mud, but he can be fun, too, Mallory."

"I know that. I think your dad is a lot of fun."

"He dressed up like Batman," Jess reminded her.

Mallory smiled at the memory. "Yeah. He did."

"And he let me keep Lucky."

"I know. He's a great dad."

"He'd be a great husband, too. And you'd be a great wife."

Yeah. She finally got why Phil was so worried. Jessica really was mapping out the rest of their lives.

"I'm sorry. It's just not going to happen. I really like your dad, but not like a husband and wife like each other."

"You don't love him."

Mallory shook her head.

"But you could. If you tried."

Damn it. Her heart was breaking right along with Jessica's. "Sweetie, people don't have to try to fall in love with each other. They just do."

Jess lowered her face. "You're not going to be my mom?"

"I'm going to be your friend. And if you ever need anything, I'm going to be there for you. That's kind of like a mom."

"Not really."

"That's the best I can do, Punk. We'll just have to find a way to make the best work for everybody."

Jess focused on her pillow, plucking at a string as her face fell into a deep frown. "Yeah. I guess."

"Have you had dinner yet?"

"No." Her pout was adorable and heart-wrenching all in one.

Mallory playfully tapped her nose. "Well, we can't have you going hungry. Should we ask Dad if I can take you to the café?"

"Can he come?"

"I think this should be a girls' night. You and me and a big pile of rainbow pancakes."

She nodded, but her usual spunk, her natural happiness, was missing.

Mallory wished she could find a better way to help her understand, but she simply couldn't. Not when she didn't fully understand the situation herself.

sh

Hours seemed to have passed from the time Mallory and Jessica had left until headlights turned into his driveway. Phil had gone from pacing the living room to scratching Lucky's ears to debating whether he should text Mallory to check in. His final attempt at a distraction was sitting with his laptop, trying to focus on work. He was feeling completely uninspired, and the draft proposal was due in two days.

Pushing himself up off the sofa, he opened the door and waited for Jessica and Mallory to come in. His first real smile all day faded when he realized that Jessica had hopped out of the car but Mallory's door had remained closed.

"Hey, Jess," he said as she ran by him into the house.

"Hi, Dad."

He looked back outside. Mallory backed out of the driveway, and his stomach clenched tight. Closing the door, he blew out his disappointment on a long breath and focused on locking the door. By the time he turned around, Jessica had toed off her shoes and was hanging up her coat.

"Good dinner?"

"Yeah."

She wasn't chattering like she usually did. Normally he had to remind her to slow down and breathe. She was still giving him the cold shoulder.

"Ready to talk to me yet?"

She faced him, her face not quite angry but looking...fed up. Yeah, he kind of felt that way, too.

"Mallory is still going to be my friend, but I don't think she likes you very much right now."

He nearly laughed, mostly at Jessica's presentation, not her words. "I'll call her and tell her I'm sorry."

"Good."

"Jess," he called when she started to leave. "You can be mad at me if you need to be, but don't forget that I love you, and even if it doesn't seem like it right now, I *always* do what I think is best for *you*."

She softened just enough that he knew she heard his words. "I love you, too, Daddy. And I am still mad at you because you hurt Mallory's feelings."

He swallowed hard. "Did she say that?"

"She didn't have to. I might be a kid, but I know when

someone's feelings are hurt."

"I didn't mean to hurt her feelings. I'll call her and tell her that. You should get in the shower. You have school in the morning. I'll come tuck you in when you're ready."

She didn't say anything else. Man, he'd really screwed this whole thing up.

Sitting on the couch, ignoring his failed attempt at working, he considered what he should say as he gave Mallory time to drive home. The last thing he needed to do was distract her while she was driving.

When he'd given her more than enough time to get home and settle in, he held his breath and connected the call. He deepened his frown with each passing ring. He'd finally accepted that she wasn't going to pick up and was piecing together the voice mail he planned to leave when she answered.

He stuttered, surprised to hear her voice. "Uh, hey. It's Phil."

"Hey." Her tone was just about as chilled as Jessica's had been.

"I just wanted to thank you for coming over and helping with Jess. I appreciate it."

"You're welcome."

"Um. So..." He stumbled again. *Apologize*, he demanded in his mind. But he said, "So how was she? Did she talk to you?"

"Yeah, she did. I told her I'd take her to a movie this weekend. I know I should have asked first, but—"

"No. It's fine," he said quickly. Too quickly. Damn, he was still sounding like an ass. "It's great."

"Is the Saturday matinee okay?"

"Yeah. Great."

"She had questions about the adoption," Mallory said. "I thought you weren't going to tell her until it was final."

"She overheard me talking. I didn't know she knew until earlier."

"Well, maybe you should talk to her about it. She's feeling a bit insecure about her place with Kara and Harry if they have a new baby."

"Yeah. I'll do that. Thanks."

Silence lingered before she finally broke it. "Seeing her so upset, I get where you're coming from. I agree that we need to be more careful of the impression we're giving her."

He felt a huge sense of relief wash through him. "I'm glad you understand."

"I also understand that you're using that as an excuse to not let me in. I hope you figure that out."

"Mallory, I—"

"Tell her I'll pick her up at noon Saturday," she stated, cutting him off. "We don't want to be late for the movie."

Before he could speak, he realized she'd ended the call. Tossing his phone onto the cushion beside him, he fell back and let out a long breath. Lucky whined and pawed at him. Phil chuckled as he realized the dog seemed to be the only one around not mad at him. Patting his head, he silently thanked the dog for not telling him he was a jerk. However, when he tried to scratch Lucky's ears, the pup huffed and wobbled away.

Plopping down on the bed Mallory had bought for him, even

Lucky seemed to be giving Phil the stink eye. He checked his watch. Jessica had a fifteen-minute limit on the shower, mostly because if he didn't remind her to get out, she'd stay in there until she used up all the hot water. He pushed himself up and knocked on the bathroom door.

"Wrap it up, Punk."

"I'm out," she called, surprising him.

She opened the door, and he was even more surprised. Not only had she gotten through the shower in record time, but she was dressed and had her hair bundled up in a towel and toothpaste bubbles at the corners of her mouth. He used his thumb to wipe them away.

"That was quick," he pointed out.

"I want to draw a picture for Mallory before bed."

Of course she did.

"I'm going to surprise her."

"She'll like that." He followed her to her room, but she turned and stared at him.

"I don't need to be tucked in tonight, Daddy. I can do it."

"Sure you can," he said, wondering if she saw through his fake smile. He held his hand out. "I'll take that towel."

She yanked the terry cloth off her hair and handed it to him.

"Brush your hair—"

"I know."

"Lights out in half an hour, okay?"

She dropped her shoulders dramatically. "It's Friday."

"Forty-five minutes," he conceded.

Her smile returned. "Thanks."

Closing her bedroom door behind him, Phil made a mental note of the time so he'd remember to check that she actually did go to bed when she was supposed to. Returning to the living room, he looked around the empty space. A few months ago, he would have loved having some peace and quiet. He'd always cherished his downtime. Being a single parent, he didn't seem to get enough of that.

Now, however, the room was too quiet. Too empty.

He was tempted to call Mallory back, to try to explain once again that he was trying to do the right thing. Unfortunately, he was having a hard time believing that himself right now.

CHAPTER THIRTEEN

*M*allory hated how her stomach turned into a ball of knots every time she pulled up to Phil's house. She wanted to be mature about this situation, but almost a week after he'd dumped her, seeing him still made her want to wrap her hands around his throat and choke him. Then bang his head against the wall.

Then kiss his pain away.

Avoiding him was definitely easier. When she'd picked Jessica up for their movie date, she'd sent Phil a text asking him to send Jess out. From the moment the girl got in the car, she hadn't stopped talking about how Lucky had gotten his cast off and how Mallory just had to see how much better he was doing.

"You're coming in, right?" Jessica asked hopefully. "To see Lucky."

Mallory cursed in her mind even as she forced a smile. "Sure thing." As she turned off the ignition, the knots in her stomach rolled again, making her feel queasy. She couldn't duck and cover every time Phil was around, and if she was as committed to Jessica as she kept insisting that she was, she was going to have to learn to deal with seeing him. Sooner was definitely better than later.

If only she could stop her hands from trembling as she pulled her keys free and released her seat belt. Jessica ran ahead of her and opened the door, yelling out to her dad that she was home. When Mallory stepped into the house, her uneasiness faded at the image of Jessica with her arms wrapped around Lucky in a bear hug. The dog was sucking up her affections, cementing the notion that the pair had become the best of friends.

"Hey, buddy," Mallory cooed when Jessica released Lucky. "Look at you." Bending down, she scratched his fluffy black ears as his eyes danced and he panted with excitement.

"Look, Mal. No cast." Jessica pointed.

"Nice. I bet that feels so much better, huh?" She patted his head and stood upright when she sensed Phil's presence in the room. Her gaze immediately met his, and that knotted-up stomach sensation returned right along with all the other urges. She forced her attention back to Lucky. "How's he getting around?"

"He has a little bit of a limp, but the vet said he should work that out once he gets some muscle tone back."

"Good."

"How was the movie?"

Jessica bounced up. "You would have loved it, Daddy. Ironman is so funny. Hey, Mal, wanna see my new drawings? I'm going to make a comic book for Super Punk and Lucky."

Mallory chuckled a little at Jessica's ability to run so many words together without seeming to need a breath. "Yeah, let me see." She grabbed Jessica's outstretched hand and followed her to her room, intentionally avoiding Phil's eyes as she passed him.

Dropping onto Jessica's bed, she admired page after page of Super Punk adventures while Jess told her the story. She offered a few tips, ideas that made Jessica's eyes light up and smile widen.

"Can we do that now?" Jessica asked when Mallory suggested she add a few more pictures. "Will you help me?"

Mallory wanted to, she really did, but the weight of knowing Phil was just down the hall made her increasingly uncomfortable. "Tell you what, let's plan an art day. A whole day just drawing and painting."

"Grandma has a studio. Can we do it at Grandma's studio?"

Ugh. Kara would probably try to corner Mallory to get details that Phil likely hadn't been willing to give. But the excitement in Jessica's eyes drowned out the dread in Mallory's gut. "Yeah. If she says it's okay."

"She will. She'll love it. Let's call her."

"Whoa, slow down, Speed Racer," Mallory teased. "I need to see when I can do it."

"Tomorrow?"

"How about next weekend? I'm sure your dad wants to hang out with you without me some this weekend, too."

Jessica didn't exactly frown, but her face definitely dimmed. "You're more fun."

Mallory teasingly tapped Jessica's nose. "Dad's fun, too. Maybe you just need to help him come up with cool ideas."

"I miss having you here," Jessica said.

"I know, Punk, but we had a good time today, didn't we?"

"It's not the same."

"I know."

She did frown then, and she lifted sad eyes to Mallory. "Do I have to wait until next weekend to see you? Can you pick me up from school one day?"

"We'll see."

"Whenever Daddy says 'we'll see,' he really means no."

"Jessica, do you think you could do me a favor? Do you think you could try to be patient while Daddy and I figure out some things? I know it's hard to understand. Grown-up problems always are."

Jessica scowled and grumbled. "He shouldn't have made you leave."

"Hey, your dad's number-one job is taking care of you. Even when it feels like he isn't, he is, Jessica."

"How is not being your friend anymore him taking care of me?"

"We're still friends."

"You're mad at him."

Mallory grinned. She couldn't deny that. "Haven't you ever gotten mad at your friends?"

"Sometimes."

"But when you're done being mad, you're still friends, right?"

Jessica nodded, but the pout on her face didn't ease up the slightest.

"Let's make a deal. I'll do my best not to be mad anymore, and you be patient and let this all work out. I'll talk to your grandma about next weekend, okay?"

"Okay."

Mallory kissed the top of Jessica's head before leaving her alone. She wanted to head right out the door, but her cold shoulder wasn't doing anyone any good. Stepping around the couch, she waited for him to lift his gaze from his laptop to look at her. "Is it okay if Jess and I hang out next weekend? She wants to do some art projects with Kara and me."

He stared at her with wide eyes. "Uhh…"

Rage instantly filled her veins. If this jerk didn't stop going from hot to cold and yes to no without warning, she really was going to strangle him. "You said I could spend time with her."

He flinched at the venom in her tone. Even she was taken aback by the bite in her words. She knew her anger at him ran deep, but in her determination to avoid him, she'd also spent far too much time replaying his rejection over and over, letting it seep into her core. Of course she was going to take that out on him the first chance she got.

"No. Yeah. I mean..." he stuttered. "Yes, you can. Just...you and my mom? Hanging out? Are you sure you're up for that?"

Oh, right. His mom. Maybe she'd overreacted. A little.

Letting out a breath, she clarified with far less edge to her tone, "Of course. We'll be hanging with Jessica."

"Uh, sure."

"I'll reach out to Kara to finalize plans."

"Thank you."

She started for the door, but he jumped up, grabbing her arm. Her heart flipped and flopped, and she immediately looked at the hallway. There was no sign of Jessica.

"Can I walk you out?" he asked, his eyes conveying that he wanted a lot more than just to make sure she arrived safely at her car.

She wanted to tell him no, but they still had things to work out. Ways that this entire situation needed to smooth out before they both caused Jess more pain than they had already. "Sure." She did make a point to pull her arm from him, though. He didn't need to get handsy with her.

Outside, he stuffed his hands in his pockets as they walked toward her car. "I know I screwed up. I'm sorry."

"I don't need an apology."

"You sure?" he asked lightly. "Because you still seem pretty pissed."

"I am. I'm very pissed."

"Jessica says I hurt your feelings."

Stopping at her car, she turned and glared at him. "You really need an eleven-year-old to explain that to you?"

"I didn't mean to."

"If you weren't committed to me and a future with me, you shouldn't have slept with me. That was a serious college-guy asshole move, Phil."

"I didn't..." Lowering his face, he at least had the decency to look ashamed. "That wasn't my intention, Mallory. I'm sorry." Lifting his gaze to hers, he looked at her with distressed eyes. "It was not my intention to make you feel used."

Anger rolled through her. "The only reason I *feel* used is because I was. At least have the courage to admit it."

He lowered his face again. "The other day, at the attorney's office, I was holding Mira while Mom talked about all the ways the baby's life was going to be better once we got things settled, and I swear, Mallory, it was like when Katrina left all over again. I was there, holding the baby, while Mom settled the legalities of her custody. There we were again, just like all those years ago, dealing with the fallout of a mother walking away. Jessica is still dealing with the fallout. I can't let her face that again."

Mallory felt like a knife was twisting in her heart yet again. "Are you comparing me to Katrina?"

His gaze shot to hers. "No. God, no. I'm just saying... I don't know what I'm saying."

Crossing her arms, she stared at him. "Look, I get that you want to protect her, Phil. She's had a tough life. She misses a mother she doesn't even know. She got the short end, and you want to make sure that doesn't happen again. I get that. I do. But I would never just walk out on her. If you don't know that by now—"

"I do know that."

"So then you did use me?"

"No. I just...we went too fast. That's all."

She looked out over the neighborhood, not really seeing the small houses and muddy spring yards. The rain and sunny weather seemed to be fighting an uphill battle. No matter how much the grass was watered and the sun shone, the yards remained dull from the cold of winter. Colors seemed to elude the scenery. Everything was dreary.

How fucking fitting.

"You know, when we first started...whatever this mess is... your back-and-forth was charming. I thought it was cute how you obviously wanted to be with me but seemed to be holding back because you have this whole *Super Dad* thing going. Guess what. It's not so cute anymore. You've been toying with my emotions—you had sex with me and whispered all kinds of sweet nothings—with no intention of going forward. You have been manipulating me long enough."

A look, something akin to panic, filled his eyes. "That's not what I've been doing."

"Really?"

"Mallory."

"Your little game of mixed signals is one I'm not interested in playing."

"I wasn't playing with you. I—I—"

"What?" Narrowing her eyes, she dared him to continue.

"I just..."

Putting her hands to his face, she forced him to look at her. That was a mistake. She instantly wanted to break down and cry the moment she breached the icy barrier she'd put between them. His eyes seemed to reflect the same pain she'd been trying to sort through.

"You're scared," she whispered. "That's okay because I'm scared, too. I've been abandoned, too. I've had my heart broken, too. But you can't hide behind your daughter for the rest of your life. It's not fair to you. It's not fair to her, and it sure as hell isn't fair to me. There is something here. Between us. You cannot deny that."

Phil's Adam's apple bobbed as he swallowed. Then he whispered, "I have to put Jessica first, Mal."

She dropped her hands as her heart hardened and her rage reignited. "Screw you if you think I'm not putting Jessica first."

"That's not what I meant."

"The only person here hurting Jessica is *you*."

"Go to hell," he breathed.

"You go to hell. And take your damned mommy issues with you."

He called her name, but she ignored him. She climbed into her car, slammed the door shut, and backed out without casting him another glance.

sh

Phil rolled his head back as, once again, his call to Mallory went to voice mail. This time he left a message, tired of calling just to be ignored.

"I don't want to have to apologize to your voice mail, but you aren't leaving me much choice. Look, Mal. I know I'm messed up. I never tried to pretend I wasn't. But I never tried to hurt you, either. I'm sorry. I didn't mean to give you mixed signals. I like you. I do. We have a lot of fun together. More fun than I think I've ever had. Maybe that's the problem," he added quietly. "I don't know what I'm supposed to do or how to be most of the time. I just know that...we all seem to be hurting right now and it's my fault. I'm sorry."

He debated whether he should say more, offer a way to fix it. But he didn't know how to fix it. So he hung up.

He'd spent so much of his life blaming his mom for everything. His dad was right about that. Nobody even seemed surprised when he dragged Kara through the mud. It wasn't intentional. Old habits, he guessed. But he couldn't blame her for this, no matter how he tried to twist things around.

Harry was right. Kara was right. Mallory was right.

Phil had issues, and until he figured them out, *he* was the one causing damage to everyone around him.

He needed to hash this out with someone, but a crazy reality hit him as he ran down the list of people he knew. Other than the guys at work, the moms in Jessica's gymnastics class, and his parents, he didn't really have anyone to talk to.

He'd been in Stonehill for a few years now. Long enough to buy a house, long enough to make sure Jessica made some friends and got involved in some activities, and definitely long enough that he should have someone to call to share his troubles with. But he couldn't think of a single person. Except one.

Tapping the screen on his phone, he texted the only person he knew he could count on to help him sort all this out. His freaking mother.

Did Dad tell you I screwed things up with Mallory?

She must have had her phone in her hand or close to it, because she called him almost immediately. "You know I hate typing on that little screen."

He smiled. "If you'd wear your reading glasses, you could see better."

"Are you okay?"

The rock that he'd been trying to deny was sitting in his stomach seemed to grow. "I don't know, Mom."

"I'm coming over."

He didn't try to stop her. He didn't try to talk her out of it. For some stupid reason he couldn't explain, he'd been hoping she'd say that. He simply sat there, waiting for her like that time when he got sent to the principal's office for correcting the science teacher. The man had completely miscategorized a chambered nautilus as a shellfish instead of as a cephalopod. He was wrong. Phil corrected him. And, in true Phil fashion, had pressed his point until he was sent to the office.

Though his mom likely didn't know if Phil was right or not, she had taken his side and even proven his point by making the principal do the research right in front of them. When the principal had to admit that Phil was right and the teacher was wrong, she had pointed out that Phil spent an entire summer on a boat learning about marine life. Of course he was right.

That wasn't the point, the man had said. The point was, Phil shouldn't correct teachers as a matter of respect. Kara had wanted to pull Phil from the school right then—she hated that he was being told to bow to authority without question—but Phil had backed down and promised to never correct a teacher again.

His mother had been livid but had honored his request that she let him stay in public school.

Even now, he had to smile at how distressed she'd been about him dumbing himself down to fit social expectations. Back then, he'd thought she was overreacting to the entire situation, but now, as a parent, he could understand that she hadn't wanted the school system to hold him back. He had those fights on behalf of his daughter on a regular basis. The school system didn't seem to understand that her disability might have held her back in some ways, but she was smart and capable. They just needed to give her the chance.

At the sound of Lucky barking, his way of announcing company, Phil got up and let his mom in just as Jessica, hair dripping wet, rounded the corner. Her face lit up as she called out to her grandma. Phil had to admit to feeling a little pang of jealousy. Jess had been cool to him for two days now. He missed her enthusiastic hugs.

"Hey, Punk." Kara swooped her up and kissed her head.

"Are you here to tuck me in?" Jess asked.

"Of course. Go finish getting ready. I'll be there in a minute." Kara turned to Phil after Jess darted off. "Your father's right. You do look like hell."

"So do you. Where's Mira?"

She grinned. "I left her screaming in Harry's arms as he looked on with fear."

Phil chuckled at the image of his father holding a fitful Mira. There seemed to be only one person in the world who could calm that baby. And she was standing in Phil's living room. "You left a crying baby?"

Stroking his cheek, she offered him a sarcastically sweet smile. "Only because baby number one needs me."

"You got that from a thirty-second phone call?"

"I got that from Harry telling me about your conversation the other morning."

"Nothing is sacred."

She winked before disappearing down the hall to get Jessica settled in. She returned a few minutes later and dropped onto his couch, one leg curled beneath her so she could face him. Taking his hand, she smiled, but sadness shadowed her tired eyes. "Mallory isn't Katrina, Phil."

Wow. Right to the heart of it. "I didn't say—"

"Sweetheart," she said without an ounce of maternal affection. "I've been with you every step of the way since Jessica was born. I was with you when your wife left. I saw how deeply that cut you."

"Not because of me, Mom. I hurt for Jess."

"I get that. I hurt for you your entire childhood. I knew how much you needed a father that I couldn't give to you. And it wasn't because there weren't options. I've met a lot of good men in my life, men who would have been wonderful father figures for you, but I was too scared of watching someone else walk out on us."

"Mom, it's not the same."

"It's *exactly* the same. Katrina left. Why would anyone else stay? You think I didn't ask myself that very question a million times when you were growing up? If your father could leave, why would anyone else stay?"

He shook his head. "It's not the same. This isn't about me."

"Okay," she conceded. "Then what is it?"

"I just don't want us to get close and then break up and Jessica to lose out on something she was counting on."

"That's a realistic fear."

"*Thank you*," he stated with the sarcasm she'd so deeply ingrained in him.

"But it isn't fair to Jessica or you. Or Mallory, for that matter. Has she done something to make you think she intends to leave?"

Phil sighed. "No."

"So maybe it is about you, hmm? Not all relationships work, Phil."

"Dad already gave me this lecture."

"But did you listen?" She tugged his hand gently. "I know you. You've picked this thing apart a hundred times in your head. Tell me what you're worried about."

He had indeed overanalyzed every bit of his relationship with Mallory. Sitting back, thinking over all the pieces, he picked one he hadn't voiced yet. "Mallory is so young."

"So are you."

"She's never had the responsibilities I've had."

"You're more mature? Is that what you're saying?"

He shook his head. "I'm just saying, maybe she thinks she's ready for a relationship with a man and his preteen daughter, but does she really know what that entails?"

Kara smiled. "Considering how much time she's been spending with you guys, I think she does. And before you bring up Jessica's disability, consider that Mallory has been learning to handle Annie's condition for a while now. She's not as inexperienced as you think." Squeezing his hands, she waited for him to meet her gaze. "Listen to me and hear what I am telling you. Jessica isn't the only one who has a hole in her life. You do, too. I see it when I look into your eyes, Phil. It's the same hollow reflection I had for so long. You've built your life around your daughter, which is admirable, but you need more. You deserve more. So does Jessica. If Mallory isn't the one for you, that's fine, but don't keep hiding yourself behind this wall."

He rested his elbows on his knees and looked at Lucky asleep on the big bed Mallory had bought for him. Memories of the day they found the mutt flooded him. Mallory had been so protective of Jessica, clearly willing to put herself between Jess and Lucky if the dog had turned out to be mean. She'd reassured Jessica over and over as they waited for the vet to give them news on Lucky's condition. Other than him and Kara, Mallory had probably been the only other person to so easily console his daughter. She was a natural with Jessica. And she was genuine.

"I just don't want to count on her and then have her change her mind," he admitted. "What if she changes her mind, Mom?"

She stroked his back. "Honey, we can't control other people. We can't predict what they'd do in the future. We also can't live our lives based on what someone else may or may not do. You have to take a chance on someone sometime. Otherwise, sweetheart, you're never going to love anyone. And how sad of a life would that be for you and for your daughter?"

Phil sank back and frowned, taking a moment to imagine his life as it had been—pre-Mallory. Did he really want to go the rest of life spending his evenings without her? Without her laughter. And did he want that for Jessica? He couldn't remember the last time she had been so happy. Yes, they had a full life, a happy life, but not like it had been the last few months.

Mallory brought something to the table that he hadn't. That element of fun, the spontaneity that his mother had given to him during his childhood. As much as he'd resented not having the stability he was trying to give to Jessica, he had to admit he'd grown up with adventure. He had amazing memories of his childhood, memories of going places and trying new things. What would Jessica remember? What would he remember of his life when he got older?

Without Mallory, it all seemed so drab. So boring.

Damn it. His mom was right. He *hated* when his mother was right.

allory hadn't laughed as much as she had sitting in Kara's studio since...well, since Phil had done his about-face and destroyed the fun they'd found in each other. When she'd arrived at Kara's house, Mallory had been on the defensive, waiting for Kara to pry into the real reason that she and Phil were on the outs. She didn't assume that Phil would have filled her in, but maybe Jessica had.

Her fears were unfounded, it seemed. While Kara had given her a few sympathetic looks when Jessica brought Phil up, she hadn't pried like Mal had expected. She appreciated the respect of her privacy and was thankful the three of them could simply be together and have a good time.

They'd spent the last hour taking turns painting images of each other, each one getting sillier and sillier. It was Jessica's turn. She flipped her picture around, showing her "portrait" of Mallory, which was really a woman with big rainbow hair riding a unicorn through the sky. The three of them burst into another fit of laughter.

Mallory had no idea where she was going to hang all these paintings, but she was determined to display them all somewhere in her home. She might even take Rainbow Mallory to her office and hang it on her wall.

"I want to paint Grandma now," Jess said, not even waiting for anyone to agree that she got another turn. She just tore off the painting she'd been doing and started another one.

"Thank you," Kara said to Mallory as Jessica focused on rinsing her brushes.

Uh-oh. Had her luck run out? "*For?*" she asked tentatively.

"For today. I really needed a distraction."

Mallory offered her a sweet smile, feeling guilty for expecting the worst from Kara. "How's the adoption going?"

"Good. Everything should be finalized soon."

"Has she…Lynn… Have you seen her?"

"Nope." She glanced at Mallory, and her eyes turned sad. "Wherever she is, whatever she's doing, I hope she finds peace in it. And never looks back. I hate to say that, but…"

"But sometimes kids are better off without blood relatives holding them back," Mallory finished.

"Yeah. Sometimes."

"How's Mira?"

Kara's smile was one of pure love. "She's getting better. We're getting her settled into a real schedule, and a lot of the tension surrounding her has eased. That's important. Kids pick up on the stress around them."

Mallory didn't think that was a jab at her and Phil, but she couldn't help but feel it. "Phil and I are working around our issues. Just so you know."

"I know." Kara put her hand on Mallory's, giving it a motherly squeeze. "Honey, you don't have to tell me what's going on. I have eyes and ears and a granddaughter who tells me everything. Just keep her best interests at heart. Phil will figure his own problems out in his own time."

Mallory nodded, deciding not to tell Kara that she had no intention of sitting around waiting for Phil to sort out his demons. His issues had hurt her enough. He could figure them out with someone else.

Jessica's giggles drew their attention. She was attacking the canvas with a paintbrush and an air of hijinks that undoubtedly would lead to another round of laughs.

"That sounds absolutely mischievous," Kara said. "Let me see."

Jessica laughed again. "No! It's not done yet." Sticking her tongue out in a show of concentration, she made several more swipes with her brush, giggled, and eyed her grandmother. "Are you ready?"

Before she shared her painting with them, Harry came rushing into the room. The raw panic on his face made Mallory's heart drop.

"Kara," he said. "Mira's burning up."

Kara jumped from her stool, running toward the living room with Harry right behind her.

"What's wrong?" Jessica asked Mallory, her eyes wide and all her happiness drained.

"I don't know." Standing, Mal held her hand out. With Jessica's fingers entangled around hers, they walked quickly, but didn't run like Kara and Harry had, toward the living room.

"She was quiet for too long," Harry was explaining as Kara fussed over the crib that had become a permanent fixture in the living room. "She's never been quiet that long."

"It's okay," Kara said, soothing her husband, but her voice wasn't convincing. "Get me cold rags."

"I'll get them," Mallory offered. "Come on, Punk. Show me where the washrags are."

"Grab the thermometer, too," Kara called after them.

"What's wrong with Mira?" Jessica asked, her voice quivering as she led Mallory to the bathroom.

"Sounds like she just has a little fever," Mallory said. "She'll be okay. Grandma will know what to do." Even as she tried to reassure Jessica, her heart continued to race with anxiety. Kara sounded worried. If Kara, a midwife, sounded worried, then maybe there was more going on than just a fever.

Jessica opened a drawer. Mallory pulled out several rags, running them under cold water and squeezing out the excess, while Jessica got a battery-operated thermometer from the medicine cabinet. "Let's take these to Grandma."

The sense of dread in Mallory's stomach grew as they closed

in on the living room, where the only sounds were Harry and Kara sounding upset as they discussed Mira's condition. Harry was right in saying that Mira was never quiet for long, especially when Kara wasn't in the room. The baby seemed to need Kara's soothing spirit near her at all times. Kara was pressing her hands all over, as if assessing her.

Something was definitely wrong.

While Kara pressed a cold rag to Mira's forehead, she held the thermometer under the baby's arm. When it beeped, she looked at Harry, her eyes wide. "She's too hot. We're going to the ER."

"Oh, no," Jessica gasped.

Mallory hugged her close. "Do you want me to drive?"

"Please," Harry said.

She followed him and Kara through the kitchen and to the garage. Harry handed Mal his keys while Kara secured Mira in her car seat. Again, the silence was unsettling. Other than Kara whispering encouraging words to Mira while Jessica sniffled, the car was silent until Mallory pulled up to the emergency room doors.

"Call Phil," Harry ordered as Kara released the buckles holding Mira in. "Have him call the attorney. Someone needs to find Lynn. We can't make decisions about Mira's care yet."

"Stay with me, Punk," Mallory ordered. "I gotta park before we go in." She pulled Harry's car into the nearest vacant spot and, hands trembling, pulled out the keys. She and Jessica climbed out and met at the back of the car. By the time they reached the reception area, Kara and Harry were being ushered back. Mallory held her breath and swallowed. She probably would have stood frozen, terrified, if Jessica hadn't sniffled beside her.

Kneeling down, she wiped Jessica's cheeks. Only then did she notice the red and blue stains on her hands from their afternoon of painting. She examined Jess's little hands and found the same. "Let me call Daddy, and then we'll go wash up."

"Is Mira okay?"

"She will be," Mallory whispered. Silently, she wondered if she was right.

sh

Phil rushed into the emergency room waiting area. He'd been building a doghouse for Lucky, excited to surprise Jessica, when he'd gotten Mallory's call. He suspected she was trying to sound calm for Jessica's sake, but he had heard the concern in her voice the moment she said his name. His stomach knotted tighter and tighter with each word. Mira was sick. He needed to call the attorney because Lynn still had parental rights. Someone had to find her.

"I'll be there as soon as I can," he'd said. Thankfully, he had a business card from the attorney in the pile of receipts and change that he piled up on his dresser when he emptied his pockets every night. He found the card fairly quickly.

The attorney said he'd meet them at the ER, but Phil didn't

see him as he rushed in. His heart melted at the sight of Jessica and Mallory huddled together on a fake leather love seat. "Is the attorney here yet?"

Mallory looked up, and Jessica jumped from her side to hug Phil.

"Mira's sick," she said, burying her face in his stomach.

He hugged her tight. "I know, Punk. I'm sure she's already starting to feel better." He lifted his questioning gaze to Mallory.

"I don't know what the attorney looks like."

He held his hand about eight inches over his head. "Tall, muscular, African American. Looks like he walked right out of the NFL and onto a *GQ* cover."

She smirked. "Oh, no. I would have noticed a guy like that. He isn't here yet."

Did she really have to say that she'd notice a guy like that with that underlying husky tone she used when they were alone? "Right." He brushed his hand over Jessica's hair. "What happened?"

Mallory shrugged. "Harry ran in while we were painting and said Mira had a fever. Kara took her temperature and said we needed to bring her in."

"She wasn't crying, Daddy. She was just lying there."

His heart tripped over itself. That kid was always fussy. "Sometimes when you don't feel good, you get quiet, too. You like to just lie around until you feel better. I'm sure Mira feels the same right now."

The concern in Mallory's eyes made him question his

reassurance. He heard his name and turned to see his parents' lawyer crossing the room.

"Wow," Mallory whispered. "You weren't kidding."

The man's suit, though clearly tailored, seemed to strain against his bicep as he held his hand out to Phil. "Where are Kara and Harry?"

"They're with the doctor right now," Phil said, greeting the man.

He smiled. "You must be Jessica." He shook her hand as he had Phil's. "I'm Alan. A friend of your grandma and grandpa. It's nice to finally meet you."

"Were you a football player?" she asked, not noticing how Phil winced. He hated when she repeated his off-the-cuff commentary about people.

Laughing, he shook his head. "I just like to exercise. Being healthy is important."

"Mira's sick," she said softly.

"I'm going to go check on her right now." He eyed Phil. "Is Lynn here?"

"Not that I've seen."

Alan moved beyond Phil to the triage nurse, undoubtedly explaining the situation. Within a few moments, he was escorted through the double doors where patients were treated.

Phil led Jessica and Mallory to the sitting area where they'd been when he came in. He was going to situate Jess between them, but she hopped onto the end of the couch, pulling Mallory to her side, forcing Phil to squeeze between Mallory and the arm of the couch. He knew better than to think that was anything but deliberate, but now wasn't the time to remind Jessica that he and Mallory weren't on the best terms.

Pulling out his phone, he texted his father, asking him to send an update when he got a chance.

"Should I take her home?" Mallory whispered.

"I want to stay," Jessica protested before Phil could answer.

"Just for a while, Jess," Phil said softly. "It could be a long time before the doctor knows what's wrong."

"I can take her when she's ready," Mallory offered.

"Thanks."

Time seemed to slow to a stop. He'd check his watch expecting hours to have gone by, but only minutes had passed. He'd check his phone, expecting to have missed a text from his father, but the silence didn't lie—he hadn't received any new messages.

The sound of a familiar voice drew him from his thoughts. Lynn stood at the receptionist's desk, asking to see her daughter. An uneasy feeling formed low in Phil's stomach. She seemed concerned, genuinely concerned. At least from where he sat.

Though she hadn't been the primary caregiver for Mira for some time, she was still her mother. She was still Mira's legal guardian. She had responsibilities, and while he was happy to see her there, he was nervous at the same time. Seeing Mira sick might be the thing that triggered her maternal instincts to kick in. This might be the moment when she recognized she had to step up and engage in the baby's life.

If so, where would that leave his parents? The adoption wasn't final. Lynn hadn't signed away her rights. The child was simply living in his parents' care until the paperwork was approved and a judge made it legal. Lynn had every right to be there. More so, she had every right to tell Harry and Kara they *couldn't* be there.

He didn't know if she would. Part of him hoped she'd snap to the reality that she was the child's mother, but if she did, that would hurt his parents. They'd never stop helping her or caring for Mira, but they'd also never stop worrying. He couldn't imagine how Kara would handle that. For his family's sake, he hoped the young woman signed whatever papers she had to sign to give Harry and Kara the power to oversee Mira's medical treatment and walk way.

Lynn disappeared through the same doors the attorney had, and Phil tried to not let his mind wander to where it was pulling him. Jessica had been Mira's age when she had to have heart surgery. Katrina had stood in a room like this, cold and impersonal, declaring that she couldn't handle being a mother. Kara had tried to calm her, to reassure her, but she'd shaken her head, her long, dark hair—like Jessica's—flying around her shoulders. She looked at Phil with sad eyes, apologized, and walked out.

He'd never seen her again. Weeks later, he received divorce papers giving him full custody. At his attorney's and mother's encouragement, he pushed back and requested Katrina relinquish her rights so they never found themselves in a position to have to run medical treatment by her. For some reason, he had expected her to push back, to realize she wanted Jessica. If not Phil, at least he expected her to want Jessica.

She hadn't. She'd signed without any kind of protest.

Phil had always resented her for that. He'd always resented the void that Jessica grew up with.

When he glanced at his daughter, though, some of the edge of his long-held anger eased. Jessica sat leaning against Mallory's side. Mallory stroked her hair rhythmically, soothingly. Jess had finally stopped looking so scared and seemed content to sit there and be comforted.

The next time the big double doors opened, Harry emerged, and Phil jumped up to meet him in the middle of the waiting room.

"Her fever's coming down. They gave her some meds. She's on an IV just in case they need to give her fluids or meds."

"How's Mom?"

"Worried," Harry answered. He opened his arms when Jessica ran up to hug him. Kissing her head, he smiled down at her. "Sorry we scared you, Punk."

"Is Mira okay?"

"She will be. They think she caught a little bug, but they're going to do some blood work just to be sure."

"That's good news," Mallory said. She looked at Phil and seemed to sense that there was more he wanted to discuss with his father. "Hey, Jess. I think we should find the cafeteria and get a drink. Sound good?"

"It's this way," Jessica said, pulling away from Harry. "I saw a sign."

After Mallory and Jessica were out of hearing distance, Phil heaved a sigh. "What about Lynn?"

Harry pressed his lips together. "She's worried. As she should be. Only two people can be in there with Mira right now. She wanted Kara to stay. I think that's a good sign. She could have kicked us out."

Phil creased his brow. "Where's Alan, then?"

"He was going to talk to the administrator. See if they will at least get me and Kara listed as guardians so we can make medical decisions if need be. God, this is such a mess." He ran his hand over his hair and blew out a breath. "Sure wish whatever is wrong with her could have waited a few weeks until the adoption was final."

Phil swallowed, trying to keep his own concern out of his voice, but he had to ask. "Think she'll change her mind?"

Harry seemed to consider the possibility before shaking his head. "No. No, I think this will remind her that she's not ready for parenthood. Kara and I have already let her know she's welcome to be a part of Mira's life if she chooses, so long as she agrees to our terms on that. She's not going to want this. Not just the responsibility, but the diapers and formula and...medical bills. She won't change her mind."

"Yeah. That's why Katrina signed her rights away."

Putting his hand on Phil's shoulder, Harry gave him a

sorrowful look. "I'm sure this is bringing up a lot of memories for you. I'm sorry."

"Don't worry about me. You focus on Mom and Mira right now."

Harry glanced toward where Mallory and Jessica had wandered off. "How are things with Mal?"

He shrugged. "Tense. Uncomfortable."

"She's a good woman, Phil. She really cares about Jessica."

"Yeah, Dad. I know."

"Had to say it."

Phil nodded behind Harry at the sight of his mother rushing through the door.

She smiled and gestured for Harry to join her. "Come on. Lynn's going to give us legal guardianship. We need to sign some paperwork so Alan can get it filed right away."

The relief on Harry's face was palpable. Though he'd insisted, clearly he hadn't been as confident as he'd tried to make Phil believe. He offered Phil a smile before joining his wife. Phil was thrilled for them. This was definitely a good sign. Now they all could focus on getting baby Mira healthy again.

Mallory hadn't intended to fall asleep next to Jessica, but sometime after agreeing to stay with her until she drifted off, Mallory had dozed as well. She woke to Phil gently shaking her. And naturally, because that was how her life went, she woke with a snort, a trail of drool running from the corner of her mouth. Licking her lips and wiping her chin, she ignored his grin as she held out her hand in an unspoken request for his assistance in sitting.

"What time is it?" she whispered after he'd pulled her to her feet.

"Almost ten."

"How's Mira?"

"Good. They released her about an hour ago."

She followed him down the hall to the living room. "And your parents?"

"They've been better but are happy Mira went home with them and not Lynn."

"I bet."

"I told them I'd come over in the morning to help out so they can get some rest. They're going to need it."

"If you want to drop Jess off at my place—"

"Actually, I was hoping you'd join us. Mom told me all about how much fun you guys had painting. Sounds like maybe she could use some more of that, and Jessica wouldn't mind having you around. Neither would I, to be honest."

She stared at him, taking in the schoolboy anxiety on his face. He looked like he'd just asked her to the prom and had no idea how she'd answer. "I can swing by. Sure."

His smile eased. "Good. Also, I wanted to thank you for taking care of Jessica," he said sincerely. "You saved me a lot of stress not having to worry about her."

"Of course."

"Mallory," he stated, giving her pause with the seriousness of his tone. "I didn't have to worry about her. Not once did I wonder if she was doing okay. That might not sound like much, but that's a really big deal for me."

"I know it is." It took a moment, but she managed a smile. "Thank you for trusting me."

"Thank you for...sticking around long enough to let me." He looked at his feet, shoved his hands in his pockets, and then looked at her again. "You know this entire situation with Lynn has been hitting a bit too close to home for me, but today...I don't know if I ever really talked about it, but we were in the hospital waiting room when Katrina left. She said she couldn't handle being a parent and she walked out. And that was that."

Mallory's heart shattered. "I'm so sorry."

"Up until today, I've been pretty torn on how I feel about Mira's adoption. I know my parents love her, but knowing how abandoned Jessica has felt, part of me really wanted Lynn to step up and be the mom she should be. Today made me see things a little differently. It really is best if Lynn walks away. Mom said Lynn was genuinely concerned about Mira, but as soon as the doctor said she'd be okay, Lynn was ready to leave. She asked Mom to call her and let her know how Mira was doing. That's not how a mom should act, Mal."

"No. It's not."

"Some people really just aren't cut out for parenthood, are they?"

She shook her head, thinking of her birth father, the one she'd never met. "My mom told me she'd help me find my father if I wanted. I don't. I really don't, Phil. Marcus might just be my stepdad, but he is the only father I've ever known. The only one I'll ever need. Kara and Harry are the only real parents Mira's ever known, and they'll give her the life she deserves. Just like you gave Jessica the life she's deserved."

He huffed out his breath. "Mal, I know I messed things up. I freaked out when I realized how much Jessica cares for you. I said some things—"

"Forget it."

"No." Shaking his head, he pressed his lips together and stared her down. "I was so far off the mark about you. But the thing is, it wasn't about you."

"I know."

"It was about Katrina. And me. Maybe even a little bit about Lynn."

"I know."

He shifted his weight from one foot to the other. "I'm trying to apologize."

She smirked. "I know."

"I didn't mean to hurt you."

She licked her lip as she took her breath. "But you did, Phil. You hurt me so much. Not just by implying that I wasn't good enough for Jessica but by treating me like I was disposable. I gave you everything I thought you wanted, and you tossed me aside like I meant nothing."

"Only because you meant too much."

She processed his excuse before rolling her eyes. "You are so messed up," she whispered.

"I'm working on it. But I'm not the only one who misses you. *Us*."

"Jessica is tougher than you give her credit for," Mallory told him. "She's already adjusting to how things are."

"I don't want her to."

Rolling her head back, Mallory shook it. "Do you even recognize how often you change your mind? I mean, it's a damn good thing you never had to pick out a prom dress, Phil."

He chuckled, which made her grin.

Her smile faded quickly, however. "I am going through a lot, too, Phil. I'm still learning to accept the extent of my mom's injuries and how to care for her without overstepping. I need balance in my life. I need...security and stability. Nothing about being with you is stable."

"I've been self-centered."

"Yes, you have," she stated, not giving him any slack. "And I don't have the energy for that right now."

"Noted." He took a deep breath. "Maybe we could start small. I'm going to spend the morning with my parents. I know they're exhausted and need help with Mira. Jess and I could use the help, too. Would you consider joining us? Just to hang out. Like we used to."

As seemed to happen where Phil was concerned, she hadn't realized how much she wanted that until he offered it. But she was hesitant. Untrusting. "You're going to be with your parents. You don't need me there."

"No. But I want you there."

"Maybe," she said. "Call me tomorrow. We'll see how I'm feeling about it then."

"Fair enough."

She started for the door, but he put his hand to her arm.

"I didn't lie. When we were together. Every word I said was true, I just…"

"Got scared," she finished.

He nodded.

"I believe you. I forgive you. But I'm not sure I'm ready to be with you again. Good night, Phil."

"Night, Mal."

CHAPTER FIFTEEN

*P*hil and Mallory walked slowly, side by side, down the beach as Jessica ran ahead with Lucky. The dog's limp was virtually nonexistent, and as Phil had long ago predicted, the two were inseparable. Now that Lucky could run and play, Jessica spent time every afternoon in the backyard throwing balls and sticks, cheering him on as he fetched them. She seemed to be completely in tune with Lucky, on some level that Phil didn't really understand.

Being on the beach where they'd found him seemed to settle them both down, though, almost as if they realized the significance of being in this place. Lucky's life had been forever changed here. It seemed as if he were reflecting on that as he looked over the water with Jessica's hand on his head.

They'd spent all day at his parents' house, helping with Mira as much as Kara would allow. She was still being overprotective of the baby, hyperaware of every sound Mira had made, but midmorning, she'd caved and let Harry drag her upstairs so they could nap. Between Jessica, Mallory, and Phil, they'd managed to keep Mira happy enough for several hours.

During those several hours, even more of Phil's deep-seated fears seemed to ease. Not only had Mallory's silly dancing and singing kept a smile on Jessica's face, but Mira seemed to tolerate her fairly well, too, which said a lot. When Kara and Harry woke up, however, Mallory was more than happy to pass Mira over and return to giving Jessica tips on her artwork.

As he and Mallory neared Jessica, Phil realized Lucky's life wasn't the only one that had changed significantly. He couldn't deny that there was a part of him that was still leery, still too scared to let go of the past, but he was determined to push that part of him down. Instead of running from what he was feeling, he intended to simply acknowledge the fear but to let the happiness outweigh the doubt.

That was something new for him. Something he was going to have to work on for some time. But standing there, staring out at the water with Mallory by his side, he committed to finding a way to move on with his life. If the last few months had taught him anything, it was that always fearing the worst was keeping him from having more in life. Not just him but his daughter, too.

As if she sensed his thoughts, his daughter looked up and smiled at him. She seemed to have forgiven his missteps as soon as she'd seen that Mallory had. From what he could tell, Jessica had brushed it all under the rug and was happy to get back to how things were. He was, too, but he was smart enough to know nothing was that easy. Mallory still had her guard up, and he didn't blame her. He'd have to find a way to prove that he was working on himself.

"Where are you?" Mallory asked, pulling him from his thoughts.

After a few hard blinks, he realized that Jess and Lucky had moved along the beach. Mallory was looking at him with concern in her eyes.

Clearing his throat, he rocked back on his heels. "I need to ask you for something."

She lifted her brows in question.

"Patience. Lots of patience."

"Huh," she scoffed. "Seems to me I've already given you that."

"You have. But I need a bit more while I sort through some things. I spent most of my life angry because I didn't have a father. Then I spent most of Jessica's life angry because she didn't have a mother. Instead of processing those situations and moving on, I clung to them. Used them as excuses to keep people at arm's length. I'm trying not to do that anymore, but it's hard to let go of something that's so ingrained. I'm working on it. I just want you to know that I'm trying to do better, and I'd like to start with you."

"That's a good place to start." She offered him a smile and then stepped around him to catch up to Jessica.

He stood back, watching, taking in the scene. When she held out her hand, Jessica took it and smiled up with so much love,

Phil's heart ached. But this time in a way that made him fill with warmth and an even deeper determination to be the man that both of them deserved.

sh

Being with Phil and Jessica was too easy. Mallory hadn't intended to spend all day Sunday with them, but by the time they left Kara's, took Lucky for a walk by the lake, and had dinner at the café, her entire weekend had been devoted to the father-daughter duo.

She guessed the next weekend would be similar, since Jessica had begged for her help painting Lucky's new doghouse. Jess was going to think of ideas that she would help Mallory execute. The doghouse was bound to turn out a hodgepodge of pinks, purples, and comic book images. It'd be perfect.

Sinking into her bed, she tapped the screen on her phone and opened her social media page. She had no intention of checking in with friends or family. She opened her own page and scrolled through the images of her with Jess and Phil. For a while, she hadn't posted anything but pictures of the three of them or at least of the scenery from their various outings.

She had so many pictures of Jessica. Some with her smiling bright, some selfies of the two of them making silly faces. But there were plenty of the three of them. Looking just like the family Phil had said he didn't want.

Now that she had given up the urge to kill him, she was

starting to see his concern. They certainly had fallen into a comfortable space that would give anyone, but most especially Jessica, the idea that they had a future together. All of them.

She could see how making love had shaken Phil to the core. Mallory had felt used, but once her anger started to burn out, she knew she hadn't been. Phil was a good guy—a scared, fumbling fool, but a good guy all the same. She knew his number-one priority was Jessica's well-being, as it should be. Mallory had just been so hurt that he would ever think that anything she would say or do would put Jessica at risk.

She couldn't possibly make him understand how much she loved that kid. She had been hesitant to even try, fearing that would give him one more reason to drive that wedge between them.

Mallory loved the safety and security of being home and close to her family, but she did tend to be a bit more reckless than she thought Phil could ever be. She'd been happy with Phil and Jess, and that was enough for her. She hadn't considered that Phil would pick that happiness apart and analyze it as he did everything.

Now that she could sit back and think, she realized she should have seen his cold feet coming a mile away. Not just because he tended to overthink but because their entire damn relationship had been hot and cold from day one. She shouldn't have needed him to pull the rug from beneath her feet. She should have known to step back long before he panicked.

Not that she was excusing his behavior. A grown man should

know better than to have sex with a woman, whispering about how much he cared for her, and then walk away and think she'd be cool with it.

She still wasn't cool with that.

But she was allowing the anger to soften enough to see his side of things. His side wasn't as cut-and-dried as hers. He had more to lose; Jessica's happiness was riding on his in a lot of ways. He had every right to be cautious and even to take a step back if he needed to.

Closing her social media page, she opened her texting app and brought up the long list of messages she and Phil had exchanged. She smiled as she scrolled through the blue and purple bubbles of text. She wasn't reading them as much as remembering the moments when her heart would flutter when her phone dinged the special chime she used to let her know Phil was messaging her.

The last few texts that had passed between them were clipped, sterile of the former teasing and playfulness. Mallory missed their teasing and playfulness. Phil was serious, but his humor was sharp, and when they first got to know each other, he'd toss deadpan comments that sent her into fits of giggles. She was always shocked when he'd relax enough to snap back. He'd relaxed a lot more as their time together progressed and his jokes eased out more often. Even so, he had a way of cracking her up that she didn't think she'd find with someone else.

With the last text read, she frowned at herself and her lingering misery. She typed a message—*I had a great time today. Thanks.*—and debated sending it. Not too friendly but enough to let him know she was thinking of him. She pressed the arrow to send the message.

Almost immediately, his special ding sounded, and her heart did that ridiculous fluttering thing again. She smiled despite herself and read his message.

Me too. Night, Mal.

"Good night," she muttered to herself. "You big, stupid man."

CHAPTER SIXTEEN

*M*allory stopped in her tracks when she spotted Phil standing in the lobby of O'Connell Realty with a bouquet of brightly colored flowers. He looked anxious, and when he smiled at her, the gesture didn't seem genuine. She had no idea what the fool was up to, but damned if the ice around her heart didn't melt a little.

"I know I'm stopping by unannounced," he said. "I was hoping you wouldn't be busy."

She glanced around the room. Miraculously, no one else seemed busy either. Marcus was poking his head out of the break room, her aunt Dianna had suddenly stopped talking and was leaning to gawk through her office door into the lobby, and Courtney, the receptionist, was glancing between Phil and Mal. Thankfully Annie was at home and not there to gawk at her as well.

"Don't you have work to do?" Mallory looked around at her

co-workers. "Don't any of you have work to do?" She caught her stepfather's gaze before he backed away. "There is no need to reach for that phone in your pocket. I'll call Mom when I damn well feel like it."

He lifted his hands as if to surrender and then cast a warning glance toward Phil before returning to his mission of refilling his coffee for what was likely his tenth cup of the day.

"I'm sorry," Phil said quietly. "I didn't realize—"

"That my family and friends are just as nosy as yours? Dianna's probably on the phone with Kara as we speak. Actually, they're probably on a three-way call with my mother."

He grinned. "Probably. But mostly because Dad knows I'm here, and I have no doubt that he told Mom two seconds after I finished telling him."

She chuckled because she knew he was right. "How's Mira?"

"Better. Thanks for asking." He held the flowers out. "I hope this is okay. I didn't know what you liked, but since you like bright colors…"

She eyed the bouquet in his hand. The big blooms were beautiful. She couldn't remember the last time someone brought her a bouquet and felt a little ridiculous at how giddy she felt accepting them. "They're beautiful. Thank you." Glancing around again, she sighed at all the eyes still on their exchange and gestured for him to follow her. Inside her office, she closed the door and set the vase on her desk before facing him. "I wasn't expecting flowers. What's the occasion?"

"Um. Well." He let an uneasy laugh leave him. "I really suck at this…"

Just like when he sent her text messages, seeing him stutter made her heart flip. His awkward foot-shifting usually meant he was going to say something that either made her smile so big her face split or scowl so hard her fists clenched. "At what?"

He puffed his cheeks up and let the air out slowly. "I miss you, Mallory."

Okay. That wasn't so bad. A bit in between the face-splitting and fist-clenching. "We spent all day yesterday together. Remember?"

"Yes," he stated with a nod. "It was great. It was…perfect."

She thought so, too. She'd arrived at his parents' house with hot pizza, bantered with Kara about her poor diet, and spent the rest of the time hanging out with Jessica. She even managed to hold Mira for a bit before the baby seemed to remember she didn't like anyone. When they were getting ready to leave, Jessica asked if they could take Lucky to the lake and begged Mallory to join them.

The walk had been so fun, mostly because she and Phil actually seemed comfortable around each other for the first time in several weeks. He had seemed lost in thought several times, which helped further soften her angry edges and led to her late text to him last night.

"I miss"—he shoved his hands in his pockets in that way he did when he was struggling to express himself—"I miss the little family that we'd become," he said.

His confession shocked her. He'd said the *F* word.

Family. He'd just called them a family.

Her breath caught, and her eyes instantly pricked as tears threatened to take hold. She blinked and reminded herself to inhale. "Family is a pretty strong word."

Meeting her gaze, he stared into her eyes. "Yes. It is. But accurate, don't you think?"

She swallowed hard. Man, she was setting herself up for a fall again. But she ignored the red flags waving in her mind, warning her to slow down. She grabbed at the invitation to take what she'd been wanting all along. "I think we could use that in a general sense."

"I've had a lot of realizations lately," he confessed, "but the biggest one is that even though we were never really together, never really a couple, we made a great one. And even if we were never really a family, we could be. Should be. Jessica deserves a family. She deserves you."

Mallory held her breath as she let his words sink in. That was what she'd been trying to tell him. But she had finally heard what he'd been telling her, too. "This can't just be about Jessica. If you only want me to fill a void in your daughter's life—"

"No," he said sternly. "I want you to fill a void in mine. I know I don't deserve a second chance, but I'm hoping that maybe you'll give me one. I can't promise to be perfect, but I promise to try."

"You silly boy," she whispered. "I never expected you to be perfect."

Stepping to her, he searched her eyes, and she suspected he was looking for permission to kiss her. She wanted that. She'd barely stopped thinking about the hot kisses they'd shared before he'd turned their worlds upside down. However, she'd be damned if she'd be so quick to give him those favors again. He'd need to earn her affection.

Shaking her head, she shot him down, despite her own longing. "You haven't even taken me out on a real date, Phil Martinson-Canton. How easy do you think I am?"

"*Well...*"

She playfully swatted his shoulder. "*Hey.*"

Wrapping his arm around her lower back, he pulled her closer. "May I take you to dinner? Maybe a movie? Without my daughter tagging along as a chaperone?"

"I'm not sure I trust you enough to be without a chaperone. I seem to recall you being a little handsy the last time we were alone."

He smiled, his dimple causing her to swoon inwardly. She'd never been so weak in the knees for anyone like she was for this man. Though she now recognized how much that put her heart on the line, she hoped she never stopped feeling the heart-racing, palm-sweating, stomach-fluttering sensation she felt when he looked at her.

From the time Phil could walk, his mother had him doing

repairs around the commune and contributing to the upkeep of their home and others. That was how things had worked in any of the communities where they'd lived—everyone pitched in. Now, as a grown man, he didn't have to think twice about how to build things like doghouses or bookshelves for comic book collections.

While Mallory and Jessica giggled and slathered paint on Lucky's new domain, Phil drilled screws into the shelf that he was building for Jessica's room. She only had four comics to put there, but she was already getting a pretty good collection of action figures and wanted a place to put the framed photo of the three of them from the comic book convention. She'd painted the wood in colors that matched Wonder Woman's outfit, which had instantly reminded Phil of the tattoo on Mallory's shoulder.

Once the shelf was complete, he snapped a picture to send to his mother along with his heartfelt thanks. She was the reason he had the skills to make the project. He knew how she'd love hearing that. In fact, she'd probably show the message to Harry as she sniffed and blinked back tears. Phil had never been good at acknowledging the good things his mom had done, but that was something he was determined to change.

As Mallory and Jessica were teaching him, everyone could complain about the past and worry about the present. Finding happiness meant finding the things he could compliment instead.

"Look at this, Daddy," Jessica called, drawing him from his introspection.

The brightly painted doghouse had the same logo on the front as Lucky from the comic books Jess and Mal had been working on together. Jessica was beaming not just with pride but with happiness. She wrapped her arm around Mallory's shoulder and hugged her.

"Didn't Mallory do a great job, Daddy?"

"Mallory did an amazing job," he agreed. Setting the drill down, he dusted his hands on his pants and walked over to take a closer look.

"This is us," Jessica said, pulling him to the side of the house where she'd drawn the three of them and Lucky sitting diligently by her side.

Seeing her draw them as a family no longer made his stomach roll in on itself. Instead, he put his hand on her shoulder and told her she'd also done an amazing job. Mallory joined them to admire the mural Jess had added, and he slid his arm around her lower back, pulling her against his side.

She looked up, clearly surprised. Though they'd agreed to try things again, they hadn't shown a bit of affection toward each other in front of Jessica. But he was doing it. Showing affection in front of Jessica. Mallory's expression of surprise faded as she smiled up at him.

She wrapped her arm around him and rested her head on his shoulder. He didn't think, he just responded and planted a kiss on her forehead.

Jessica, never one to miss a thing, gasped. "Daddy," she whispered. "You're hugging Mallory."

Laughing lightly, he nodded and pulled Jessica closer, too. "Yeah, I am, Punk."

He didn't think she could have looked any happier than she had talking about the doghouse, but her eyes seemed to fill with even more light.

"Is she your girlfriend now?" Jessica asked.

Phil glanced at Mallory. She raised her brows in question, too. Phil nodded. "Yeah. Mallory's my girlfriend now."

Jessica threw her arms up. "Yes! It's about time!" Wrapping her arms around them both, she rolled her head back. "This is going to be awesome."

Mallory's eyes filled with the same happiness that had shined in Jessica's. The same happiness filled him, wrapped around his heart and, to his amazement, seemed to mend all those shattered bits he'd refused to let heal. He felt whole for the first time, maybe in his entire life. He felt whole *and* happy.

Cupping Mallory's cheek, he grinned. "This is most definitely going to be awesome."

EPILOGUE

*J*essica held Mira back, not letting her stick her tiny fingers in the icing on the cake. One candle burned bright as the crowd sang out "Happy Birthday" to Jessica's much younger aunt. Mira wasn't quite as fussy as she used to be, so she sat still as Jess hugged her and beamed proudly, almost like it was her own birthday.

The truth was, she had shown up at this party determined to hold Mira. She thought Grandma probably wanted to be the one to help the birthday girl blow out her candle, but Jessica was on a very serious mission.

Mira wasn't old enough to know how to use her birthday wish, but since Jessica was going to be blowing out the flame, she thought she'd probably be able to put her own spin on it.

As the song came to an end, Jessica took a big breath, hugged her aunt tight, and blew as she thought the one thing that she'd been thinking ever since her dad and Mallory decided to become a couple—*I wish I was a big sister.*

Jenna Reid jumped back as water shot straight out of the pipe leading to her kitchen sink. She screamed, dropping the wrench when an ice-cold deluge soaked every inch of her body crammed under the industrial-sized sink. She covered the open joint with her hands but, like a fire hydrant struck by a wayward car, the stream was too powerful to be contained. Water squirted through her fingers and drenched her face.

She could have sworn she'd shut off the water, but apparently, she could add the valve to the list of things that didn't work in the broken-down kitchen of her broken-down diner. She held her breath and turned her face away as she assessed the situation, determined not to let panic set in.

She had to figure out why the valve hadn't turned off. If she didn't, she'd have to sit there holding the pipe while water sprayed her face until someone—likely her brother Marcus—came to her rescue.

She was done letting other people save her. She was an adult. A full-grown woman, damn it. She could do this. She could fix this.

She pulled herself up and shrieked, her tennis shoes skating across the wet cement flooring as she rushed toward the shut-off valve on the other side of the wide sink. She dropped to her knees and turned the handle as hard as she could. But once the valve was off, the water didn't stop. She turned the lever the other way.

Water continued flooding the cement floor.

"No," she begged. "No, no, no. Goddamn it!"

Despite her efforts, the puddle continued to grow.

The valve clearly wasn't working.

Rushing back to the sink, she slid to where she'd loosened the joint and fumbled with the pipe wrench. If she got the...*thingie-ma-jig*...tightened, maybe the water would quit spraying the entire room and she could clean up and pretend this never happened.

Then Marcus could fix it—like he'd told her *he* would. She could be grateful and repay him with dinner—like she'd told him *she* would before she decided watching a video on YouTube qualified her to be her own plumber.

The only problem—okay, not the only problem, but the biggest problem—was the pressure seemed to be increasing. The water was shooting faster. And she was certain the temperature was even colder than before. Whatever she'd done to the valve was making things worse.

A scream of frustration ripped from her as the frigid torrent made it even more difficult for her fingers to operate. Her heart pounded in her ears, nearly obscuring the constant *whishing* of water coming from the pipe. Her eyes blurred, but she wasn't sure if it was tears of defeat or water draining from her hair into her eyes. She fumbled with the pipe wrench, trying to redo what she'd undone when she'd decided to replace the section of leaking pipe, saying words that she was sure would shock most people who knew her. Jenna tended toward the innocent side of things, but she certainly had it in her to drop an F-bomb or two if the occasion called for it.

And that occasion was now, as she sat saturated on the kitchen floor of the diner that was falling down around her faster than she and her brother could duct tape it back together. She was about to let another curse rip when, without warning, the geyser turned to a trickle.

Finally, her kitchen was silent save for her desperate panting and the annoying *ping-ping-ping* that had started this entire fiasco.

The non-stop drip had been going for days. Marcus had told her what he needed to do to fix it; he'd even bought a new section of pipe and fittings. He just hadn't had the time to devote to her plumbing. Tired of hearing the sound of droplets clinking in the metal bowl she'd put under the sink, she'd decided to be her own hero.

"Way to go, genius," she muttered.

Wiping her forehead—which was pointless since her hands

were as soaked as her face and the strands of dark air sticking to it—she sat back on her heels and choked down the sob that was threatening to erupt.

"Are you okay?"

The unexpected male voice caused her to jolt. A squeal eeked out of her as she lurched back. She wobbled for a moment then landed on her ass in the pool that had formed behind her. A man emerged from the shadows on the other side of her kitchen. Her heart seemed to stop beating as she scurried back and reached for something, *anything*, she could use to protect herself.

Bowls crashed around her as she grasped a firm handle and held up...a colander. She would have laughed if it weren't for the fact that she had no other weapon within reach. Instead, she lifted the perforated bowl in warning—if he didn't back off she'd...*strain* him. "Who—who are you?"

"I was outside. Heard you scream. Thought there might be trouble." He lifted his hands as if to prove he meant no harm. "You turned off the wrong valve."

She swallowed. He spoke slowly, in a deep voice with a hint of an East Coast drawl. He wasn't from Stonehill. Just about everyone knew everyone in this small town and she didn't know him.

His skin, what she could see of it around the dark, shaggy hair, was tan from too much sun. Like he'd worked outside most of his life. The question where he was from formed in her mind but stuck in her throat. That didn't really matter at this point in time. She sat there, letting ice-cold water soak into her jeans and numb her skin as she threatened him with fine mesh.

"You turned off the valve to the faucet, but you should have turned off the main valve," he explained. "Rookie mistake."

As he came into the light, she could see that his clothes were dingy and worn. His beard was full, but not trimmed, and his hair was shiny, as if he had gone too long between washing the strands that hung over his ears.

She couldn't determine if he was homeless or just too old to pull off hipster. Either way, he'd somehow appeared in her kitchen without her noticing, and that unsettled her.

She lifted the colander when he took a full step toward her. "This may not look deadly, but I could still put your eye out with it."

He lifted his hands, again showing his innocence, and smirked behind his facial hair.

"I have no doubt that you could. But I can help. If you want. Or you can try again now that the water's off. Whichever works for you. But either way, you might want to get out of that puddle and into dry clothes. Your lips are turning blue."

Jenna finally inhaled and looked at the clothes clinging to her. If it weren't for the vintage print of Barry Manilow's face clinging to her chest, she could have just auditioned for a wet T-shirt contest. While holding a flimsy bit of steel to save herself.

What the hell was she doing? What in the actual hell did she think she was doing?

She wasn't a plumber any more than she was a business owner.

She'd been winging it for almost three years now, but she was tired. Exhausted.

And she sure as hell wasn't capable of assaulting a grown man with a strainer. If he wanted to slit her throat and rob her...

Marcus had told her a hundred times to lock the kitchen door even when she was cleaning up. He'd told her a hundred times to carry the pepper spray he'd bought for her. He'd told her a hundred times to take basic self-defense classes.

She'd done none of those.

Not only was she ill-equipped to fix her plumbing, run a business, or protect herself, but she was also freezing. A shiver ran through her as she realized just how much water her clothing and hair had absorbed.

She laughed to stop herself from crying.

ABOUT THE AUTHOR

As a teen, Marci Bolden skipped over young adult books and jumped right into reading romance novels. She never left.

Marci lives in the Midwest with her husband, kiddos, and numerous rescue pets. If she had an ounce of willpower, Marci would embrace healthy living, but until cupcakes and wine are no longer available at the local market, she will appease her guilt by reading self-help books and promising to join a gym "soon."

Visit her here:

www.marcibolden.com

 facebook.com/MarciBoldenAuthor

 twitter.com/BoldenMarci

instagram.com/marciboldenauthor

CPSIA information can be obtained
at www.ICGtesting.com
Printed in the USA
LVHW090108260321
682548LV00008B/76